RUBOUT AT THE ONYX

M

H. PAUL JEFFERS

NEW HAVEN AND NEW YORK
TICKNOR & FIELDS
1981

Library of Congress Cataloging in Publication Data

Jeffers, H. Paul (Harry Paul), 1934–
Rubout at the Onyx.
"A Joan Kahn book."
I. Title.
PS3560.E36R8   813'.54   81-5709
ISBN 0-89919-046-4   AACR2

Designed by Sally Harris / Summer Hill Books

Printed in the United States of America

S 10 9 8 7 6 5 4 3 2 1

This book is dedicated to Thomas and Margaret Jeffers,
who were optimistic enough and so much in love with
life and each other that not even the difficult times
of the Great Depression could keep them from having
their fifth child, a son, who wrote this book.

"The music goes round and round..."
—song lyric, 1935

Contents

1

Death of a Punk

Looking back, the 1930s all come together in the rubout of a two-bit mobster named Joey Seldes at the Onyx Club, the best jazz joint on Fifty-second Street. It happened on New Year's Eve at the end of the first year after the repeal of the Volstead Act. The night had been shaping up as the biggest blast on The Street since it went legitimate. The word was out that the jazz would be very hot. Before the night got very old, Joey Seldes wandered in. Art Tatum had been flooring everyone with his incomparable waterfall crescendos at the piano during an intermission, but the band was into a second set when two hoods who'd driven up in a black Packard strolled into the Onyx knowing exactly what they were doing and opened fire with pistols before Joey had a chance to figure out what was happening.

I was not there when they blasted Joey. I'd been up The Street at Jack and Charlie's 21, although everyone knew I could be counted on to be back in time for the serious jamming by the band. I wasn't surprised to learn that Joey Seldes was rubbed out, but I never expected to be the one to prove to all of us that Joey Seldes was a more ambitious punk than anybody ever realized.

Before Joey was gunned down, there had been two memorable events at the Onyx which I had been part of. There was the long night of waiting for Utah to put Repeal over, and there was the time gangster Owney Madden commanded me to take part in the greatest jam session The Street of Jazz had ever witnessed. I was by no means a professional jazzman. I was just an ex-cop who'd traded in his badge for a private investigator's license. I had a small office upstairs in the brownstone where the Onyx was, a little room at the back of the top floor, but mostly I did my business at the Onyx bar or out on Fifty-second. Those who saw me saw a big shambling red-haired ex-cop who would just as soon leave the private shamus work to someone else if there came a chance to sit in on a good jam where a non-pro Irish ex-cop clarinet-playing private eye could get in a few licks. That was the great thing about the Onyx. It was okay for a guy like me to jam with the greatest.

On the night Joey Seldes was shot, the music was going again by the time I walked into the club and over to the bar, having to almost step over Joey's body lying in a puddle of blood and covered with his overcoat while two guys in white from Roosevelt Hospital were getting the corpse ready to be moved out. The Onyx's bartender, a savvy guy named Louie, was in the middle of telling me what had happened when an inspector of the N.Y.P.D. came out of the men's room at the back of the club, spotted me, and sauntered over.

His name was Mike Grady. We'd been cops together, but we never hit it off during my years on the force. For me, Grady was sand in your shoes or fingernails on a blackboard. A hard-nosed cop, he looked the part: well over six feet tall, a yard wide, thick around the middle, flinty-eyed. I never knew Mike Grady to do anything but take everything seriously.

He cocked back his snap-brim fedora, leaned against the bar, clasped his ham-hock hands over his big belly, and cracked, "Turn up a cheap killin' in a cheap dive and you turn up a cheap private eye scroungin' around to see if there might be a buck to be made out of it."

"Nice to see you, too, Grady," I replied.

"What brings you around, MacNeil? The smell of the blood or just the smell of possible dough to be made?"

"The music brings me, Grady. Only the music."

"Ah, so you're not like one of those shyster lawyers who go chasin' after ambulances in hopes they can turn a dollar by connin' a grievin' widow into hirin' them to '*investigate*.' "

Behind the bar, Louie chimed in. "From what I hear about Joey Seldes's wife, she wouldn't need any help. A tough and independent lady."

"Lady?" Grady grunted. Then he gave a half nod toward the coat-draped corpse. "Any idea who'd want to bump Joey Seldes?"

"He probably crossed someone in his gang," I said.

"Mebbe," said Grady.

"Why don't you just haul him out of here? He's beginning to cast a pall," I complained.

"A hard case, ain't you, MacNeil?"

"Yeah, I guess I am sometimes."

"Were you here when Joey got bumped?"

"Nope."

"I thought you was a regular in this dump."

"You know I've got an office upstairs."

"Did Joey come in here much?"

"Time to time."

"Were you and him pals?"

"Shit, no."

"No offense, Harry. I just figured that since you've been workin' the streets—and the gutters—you'd probably be chums with scum like Seldes. See ya, Harry."

He swaggered away from the bar in a way he had of letting you know when he thought he'd gotten the better of you, had the last word, gotten in the last dig. If he knew I was staring daggers at his back, it would only have made him feel prouder of himself. A couple of minutes later he left, taking with him the guys from Roosevelt, the rest of his cops, and the corpse. I leaned on the bar after they'd gone and said to its genial tender, "Louie, I've got a bad taste in my mouth. Scotch'll take care of it nicely."

Louie studied me as he set up the drink, so I braced myself for one of his comments on the way of the world. Instead, he asked, "What's between you and Grady? Why's he always think he has to bust your balls?"

I swigged the scotch. It had been good scotch at the Onyx bar even when the stuff had been made down in a cellar somewhere.

I considered telling Louie the whole story of me and Grady, but instead I just set down my glass, wiped my mouth with the back of my hand, and said, "We were police precinct locker-room trouble a long time ago. It'd be boring to a civilian."

Louie nodded his bartender's nod of understanding and let the matter drop.

I glanced over my shoulder to where Joey'd been killed and said, "Hell of a way to ring out the old year, eh?"

2

The Cradle of Jazz

The club where Joey Seldes was gunned down was not the original Onyx. The first had been opened up The Street at number 35, on the parlor floor at the back of a brownstone. You got there by going down a couple of stone steps to a basement door that was always open. Inside, you went through a short hallway to another flight of steps and then up to a silver-painted doorway. You'd knock and a guy would look out through the peephole in the door. If he knew you or you spoke the right word, you got in. Inside, the original Onyx was as garish as its door, the walls alternating stripes of black and silver, the bar with a black marble top, which is where the Onyx got its name. I was in this speakeasy and listening to the Five Spirits of Rhythm, as hot a group of Negro musicians as you could find anywhere in town, including Harlem, when Utah put Repeal over at 33½ minutes after 3:00 A.M., Mountain Time, on December 5, 1933.

Joey Seldes had been there with a couple of young guys I didn't know. They were all acting tough, as if they owned the town. They swaggered out before whale-mouthed Leo Watson started scat singing and Virgil Scroggins used a whisk broom to tease a paper-wrapped suitcase that served as a drum. The whole joint began swinging. Everybody knew they were part of something historic while we waited for John Barleycorn to go legal again after the miserable failure of the insanity that someone had called "the great experiment." Nobody at the Onyx knew exactly what lay in store after that historic night, except that booze would be legit again, effective right away, as soon as Utah voted Repeal.

The guy who owned the Onyx was genial Joe Helbock, who started in the booze business bootlegging in 1927 with a telephone answering service and a couple of kids running the stuff to the clients who called up. Helbock used to brag he could age a bottle of the hooch between the time you called and the boy went out with the package. The booze business brought Helbock into contact with show-business people and musicians; and when he decided to open a speak of his own, he wanted a spot that musicians would like. He'd seen how successful Plunkett's was on Fifty-third, a dark and narrow joint west of Broadway where the Ninth Avenue el turned. Helbock palled around with Paul Whiteman and Jimmy Dorsey and noticed that musicians liked to do their business in bars and cafes; so when he decided to open a club of his own, he wanted to make it one musicians would like. That meant getting good sounds in his place, which is how the Onyx opened up Fifty-second Street to jazz. Pretty soon that's just how Fifty-second between Fifth and Sixth was known. The Street. The Cradle of Jazz.

When there was booze and money and success, the mobsters were there, too, so The Street was a place for music *and* mobs. In that, The Street was no different from other parts of Manhattan. The booze and muscle boys had been connected with clubs from the moment the country went dry, although it wasn't a gangster who got the honor of being the first New Yorker to go into the pokey for violating the Volstead Act. On October 30, 1919, a Greenwich Village innkeeper named Barney Gallant got thirty days because he continued to serve booze at fifty cents a shot at his Greenwich Village Inn. His illustrious clientele in the form of Eugene O'Neill, Theodore Dreiser, Edna St. Vincent Millay, and others got up a petition to the judge to cut the thirty-day rap in half. Gallant later opened a club named after himself on West Third Street with scotch at sixteen dollars a quart and champagne at twenty-five.

The gin joints sprang up everywhere, but Fifty-second was

always the wettest street. One night, humorist Robert Benchley made a personal census of The Street, counting thirty-eight joints while having a drink in practically every one. Benchley and his literary crowd favored Jack and Charlie's 21 or Tony's, operated by Tony Soma, who could sing operatic arias while doing yoga on his head. Tony's and 21 were for the elite, I figured, and I went there only for business.

All the clubs had to have arrangements to keep open, either with mobsters or with the cops or both. In midtown, the mobsters that speakeasy owners dealt with were under the control of Owen Owney the Killer Madden. When Jimmy Walker was Mayor and Madden was at his peak, newspaper columnist Ed Sullivan said, "You just have to ask Owney for anything you want and you get it—protection, special favors, and that kind of stuff. It's like knowing the Mayor to know Madden." Truth was, if you knew Madden you didn't have to know the Mayor.

The only mobster with more muscle was Lucky Luciano, who owned all the hookers, the gambling, and the dope in town, and to whom all the other mobsters, such as Owney, paid their respect and their tributes. Luciano was a nasty ape who tried to put on the slick sophistication that came naturally to a guy like Owney. Luciano thought he could buy class by living at the Waldorf, by wearing $500 suits and by hiring classy-looking women to go out with him.

Owney was a little guy who didn't have the ugly knife scars and suspicious, drooping eyelids of Luciano, and Owney was a guy who could relax at a club and enjoy the music instead of always trying to look tough. Not that Owney wasn't tough. He'd been a crook, killer, and gangster all his life and boasted that he'd never worked a day of honest toil in all of his forty-three years. Through the 1920s, Owney was the boss of the speaks, teamed up with Dutch Schultz in battles with Legs Diamond, Waxy Gordon and Mad Dog Coll. Owney was smart, too. He knew Repeal was coming and had been gradually shifting his interests from illegal booze to legit clubs and to the boxing rackets in partnership with Bill Duffy. Their big attraction was a South American cream puff named Primo Carnera, a giant no-talent who earned the heavyweight championship only because Owney Madden was in his corner.

By the time Repeal was in, Owney was getting weary of the mobs and thinking about retiring, especially when the cops started leaning on him, sending him away briefly in 1932 for parole violation. Owney laid low in Hot Springs, Arkansas, but returned home from time to time to keep an eye on his joints, his gang, and his rivals. He also came back for the jazz on The Street.

In 1933, La Guardia was elected on a fusion ticket, and knowing him didn't get anybody any privileges. The night he was elected he told his happy supporters at a party at the Astor Hotel that he was an ingrate and that if they thought backing him would get them an edge at City Hall they had another think coming. Less than a month later, Repeal was a fact, and the illegal booze business that had made mobsters possible was suddenly legit. Fiorello La Guardia soon was letting it be known he intended to make war on the mobs if they intended to stay in business in New York. One of his chief targets was Owney, the jazz-loving mobster who made it possible for me to have a moment of glory with the greatest names in jazz.

Owney was celebrating being sprung from Sing Sing and was at his usual table listening to the piano-playing of Art Tatum in the intermissions between the performances of the Spirits when the jam got under way. Before long, Tatum and Watson were joined by Tommy and Jimmy Dorsey, who happened to come in with Paul Whiteman. A few other musicians dropped by. Then others. And a historic jam session was under way. At the height of it, I walked in; and when there was a momentary lull, Owney spied me at the bar and yelled over the din, "Hey! The Mick Dick plays clarinet, don't he?" Owney knew I did. It was his way of suggesting that I step up with the band and join the session. Owney's suggestions were usually commands, so someone handed me a clarinet.

Joe Sullivan had taken over from Tatum at the piano. Jack and Charles Teagarden were in the group. Dick McDonough was on guitar and Manny Klein on the trumpet. Later the Dorseys reprised and Bunny Berigan wound up on trumpet while Frankie

Chase and Bud Freeman alternated on tenor sax. The jam went on to the wee hours, each man taking his lead, picking the melody apart and putting it back together his way, developing it, turning it into something new and to be heard. The word got out on The Street and pretty soon you couldn't've gotten into the Onyx if you had La Guardia with you. When it broke up, everybody said I'd held my own pretty good with all those jazz greats, so I owed one to Owney Madden, even if he was a hood and deserved to be back in Sing Sing.

Joey Seldes had been there than night, because Joey had always been a hanger-on with the Madden mob. He was a little guy with a face like a ferret's and shifty eyes; but he often had a knockout of a dame on his arm, and why he was able to do so well with women was always a mystery to me. He was a sharp dresser, although his clothes seemed a little fruity to me, and I never felt comfortable when I was around him; but Joey visited the Onyx as much as I did, although for different reasons. With him it was a spot to pick up dames, who came there to hear the jazz. I favored the Onyx because of the music and because I liked the owner and most of the guys who worked in the place, having known all of them from days long before the Onyx was opened on Fifty-second Street.

Some of the best speaks had been on Forty-ninth Street until the Rockefellers gobbled up all the property and began knocking places down to make room for Rockefeller Center. Dispossessed, the speak owners looked for new territory. The bottom having dropped out of the stock market, a lot of the town houses on Fifty-second had been put up for rent or sale, although some stalwarts hung on even after the speaks began standing shoulder to shoulder along the block in a neighborhood that once copied its style from the pile of stone put up by the Vanderbilts at the corner of Fifth Avenue in 1881. A parade of brownstone town houses sprang up along the block, more modest than the Vanderbilts' but just as quiet, dignified, and respectable, until the stock market crash. Prohibition, and the arrival of Rockefeller Center changed everything.

Most of the houses became speaks, honky-tonks, and jazz

joints. Somehow it seemed right to mix jazz with bathtub gin and bootleg scotch in cramped, smoke-filled, and noisy rooms upstairs, downstairs, or in the cellars of the converted houses. In all of them—Jack and Charlie's, the 3 Deuces, Downbeat, the Famous Door, Jimmy Ryan's, Kelly's Stable, Hickory House— New York's swells rubbed elbows with politicians, gangsters, dopesters, and musicians and guzzled booze to the accompaniment of throaty saxes, wailing clarinets, brassy trumpets, slide trombones, and rippling pianos. You used to have to go to Harlem for jazz like that until the Onyx brought it downtown in style, first in that parlor floor in the rear of the house at number 35; then, after Repeal, as a legit joint at number 72 on the south side of The Street near Sixth Avenue.

When I learned that there was some space going begging upstairs, I rented it for an office and furnished it with a second-hand desk I picked up down on Canal Street, a file cabinet borrowed from the Onyx, two chairs, a phone, and a beat-up leather couch which came in handy for having dames up from the Onyx. My sign said HARRY MACNEIL, INVESTIGATIONS. A client who happened to wander into the Onyx looking for me would just as likely be told that the "Mick Dick" was four flights up in the back, unless the client was a good-looking woman, in which case she got the specially polite treatment from the Onyx boys. "Mr. MacNeil's suite of offices is on the top floor just at the back. May we show you the way?"

Gloria Seldes skipped the polite offers and found her own way up the stairs to my office. The whole place would go up in flames only a few days after her visit, but that was in the future as she asked me to see if I could find out what really had happened, and why, to the punk whose only claim to fame prior to December 31, 1934, was in the selection of a wife.

3

Client

It was late in the afternoon on a frigid day early in February 1935 when she walked into my office and tossed off her fur coat as if she were about to pose for *Vanity Fair*. She was a real looker in a red clinging dress and a red Greta Garbo hat with a veil. The hat tilted to the right, low over her eye, forcing her to hold her head cockeyed to see me as she paused in the doorway. "You're MacNeil?"

"I am." I nodded from behind my desk.

"I am Gloria Seldes, Joey's wife."

"I know."

"May I come in?"

"Please do."

She closed the door and came over to a wooden chair by the desk. She sat so the red dress showed plenty of leg. "Joey talked about you a lot."

"Is that so?"

"He said you were a man who could be trusted. He told me that if I ever needed help, you were a good man to keep in mind."

"And now you think you need help?"

She took a handkerchief from her purse and dabbed a tear from her eye, smudging her eye makeup. She was just enough past thirty to believe that makeup could make her look twenty-five again. She tinted her hair, which made it an unattractive rusty color instead of her natural brown, worn up. She'd have been smarter to keep it natural and down, I thought. Her figure was fine—big in the breasts and wide in the hips and a pair of legs that could do things to a man. She'd been a dancer, I recalled Joey telling me. I was never clear whether Gloria had been just a dancer or a stripper. I let myself think of her as a stripper as she shed a couple of tears while telling me about how her husband had been gunned down at the Onyx. She now and then had a little catch in her voice as she spoke, which made the tears seem a little more genuine. "Mr. MacNeil," she began with a catch in the voice, "you perhaps remember the incident just downstairs in which my husband died?"

"I do," I replied, rocking in my swivel chair. "As a matter of fact, I arrived at the Onyx just after it happened. I'd been up the street at Jack and Charlie's Twenty-one having a drink with a client. So I didn't see the shooting myself. What I heard was, two men pulled up in a black Packard, came into the club, walked right up to Joey, and let him have it point-blank. Then they turned and walked out as if nothing unusual had happened. Very professional job. The cops never cracked the case."

"The police say they made a thorough investigation, but they didn't."

"How do you know that?"

"They didn't talk to any of the witnesses. They didn't talk to anyone who could have helped. They pretended to investigate. Now, they've dropped it. I got a call from Inspector Grady. He phoned and said that it was very unlikely they'd ever find out who did it and why. Grady said it was not uncommon in such cases."

"True." I nodded.

She brightened through the tears. "Yes. You were a policeman once, I recall."

"Twenty years. Never got to be an inspector though. Just a plainclothes unpolitical flatfoot."

"There was a cloud of some kind over your leaving the police?"

"That's *my* history. We're talking about yours and Joey's."

"I didn't mean to pry."

"It's all right." Ripping open a pack of Luckies, I offered her one. Lighting it for her, I said, "You knew that Joey was a mobster. You knew he worked with the Madden gang. You must have expected that something like that would happen to him. I'm sorry to be blunt, Mrs. Seldes—"

"Gloria, please."

"Gloria. You knew Joey was mixed up with gangsters."

"Yes."

"I'm not surprised that Grady's gotten nowhere on the case, so why should you be?"

"I don't think the police want to solve the case."

"Now, Gloria, why would you think that?"

"It's just a feeling. A suspicion. An intuition."

"Based on what?"

"Joey never gave any indication that he thought his life was in danger."

"He probably didn't know."

"Oh, he always knew when things were hot. Everybody laughed at Joey and said he was a flunky and nothing more, but Joey was a smart man. He knew more than other people thought he did. He never let on about a lot of the things he knew. He knew about who was going to get rubbed out and who was going to be taught a lesson. Joey had very good connections, even though he wasn't a big man in the gangs. I always knew when he was worried or when he was carrying around information that was dangerous. On the day that he was killed, he was in very good spirits. He was happier than I ever saw him. He was on top of the world. We were talking about taking a vacation at Niagara Falls, because we'd never had a proper honeymoon. He said everything was right with the world as far as he was concerned."

"Mobsters have long memories, Mrs. Seldes. Gloria! Joey was probably hit because of something long ago and long forgotten."

"I thought of that possibility, too, until yesterday."

"What happened yesterday?"

"I was going through Joey's things. I'm preparing to move from the apartment Joey and I lived in to a smaller one, and I was going through things to see what could be thrown out. I was going through Joey's closet and his things, and I was looking in pockets and the like."

"And what did you find?"

"First I found a newspaper clipping from the *Daily News* one day last December, just after Christmas. I brought it with me. Would you like to see it?"

"That's why you brought it, darling."

It was a huge headline from the front page and additional columns from inside pages written by a pal of mine, Ben Turner, about the disappearance of a man named Shmuel Kipinski, an elderly diamond and gem dealer who operated a business on Forty-seventh Street. "Mr. Kipinski," said the *News*, "had left his office to keep an appointment at the Royalton Hotel on 44th St. with jeweler Edward Carmichael of Indianapolis, Ind. Mr. Kipinski never kept the appointment. Somewhere in the three and a half blocks between his business and the hotel, Kipinski vanished."

Vanishing with Mr. Kipinski, Ben Turner reported, was a little leather sack of unset diamonds which Mr. Kipinski's partner told police were valued at three million dollars, easy.

I slid the clipping across the desk to Gloria Seldes. "So? You think Joey had something to do with this? It's a little out of his league, isn't it?"

"In the same pocket with that clipping," said Gloria, "I found other things. This gun."

It was a beauty. A .45-caliber Colt Government Automatic pistol. I sniffed the muzzle. "It's been fired," I said, checking the clip. "Twice."

"It was not like Joey to carry a gun, as you may know."

"Yeah. What else did you find?"

"A very peculiar note in Joey's writing."

"May I see it?"

"This is it."

The handwriting was crude, like a schoolboy's. The note said:

The key man is Kenny Lambda It is No. 123 in corner Mr Zero goes left To 45 twice R 36 You are Left with 85 in the corner at the back is the richest jock in town Mr Z is the man to see on 47 when it is safe

"What do you make of it?" I asked Gloria Seldes.

"If I could make anything of it I wouldn't come to you, would I?"

"Maybe you would, maybe you wouldn't. What do you want me to do? I'm not a guy who makes it his everyday business to crack codes, you know."

"It's a code, then?"

"Seems obvious to me. It's a combination to a safe, among other things less obvious. Does Joey have a safe?"

"A safe? Joey never had anything worth putting into a safe, believe me. How do you know it's a safe combination?"

"Easy. Zero, left to forty-five, then twice right to thirty-six, and left to eighty-five."

"You're very clever, Mr. MacNeil."

"Harry."

"Harry. I'd've never figured that out."

"It'll do no good to know the combination of a safe unless you know where the safe is. You don't have any idea?"

"None."

I looked at the note again. "This guy Kenny Lambda. You know him?"

"I never heard the name."

"What about Mr. Z?"

"No."

"Of course, that could be a code, too. The forty-seven could be Forty-seventh Street, where this jeweler was grabbed and disappeared. Could be the forty-seventh floor of a building, too. Empire State maybe. Or the Chrysler Tower. Or the RCA Building. A couple of buildings with forty-seven floors. Could also be a date. Four-seven. April seventh. Any of that mean anything?"

She shook her head and patted her upswept rusty hair. She had a tear again and the little catch in her voice. "Do you think Joey had something to do with the disappearance of that diamond man?"

"I can't say. Is that what you want me to find out?"

"It could be why Joey was killed. I loved Joey very much, Mr. MacNeil."

"Harry."

"I loved him and I want whoever killed him punished."

"The odds on that are not very good. I have to tell you that before I ask you for money. It'll take money to look into this. I get fifty bucks a day and expenses. I don't work cheap. If you work cheap, you work a lot. If you're dear, you don't work as hard and the money is the same. If you want someone cheaper, I can call a friend who's available. Good man, though."

"Joey had insurance. It just paid off. That's why it's taken me so long to come to you. I was waiting until I had money. I know you're a professional investigator and that probably you wouldn't look into Joey's murder without money, even though you have an interest in solving the murder. A personal interest, I mean."

"Beg pardon? What personal interest?"

She gave me a look that was as amazed as I felt. "Well, Joey visited you that night when he was killed."

"Wait! Joey never came to see me that night. Only thing I saw of him was him under his overcoat. What gave you the idea he saw me that night?"

"He told me he was going over to the Onyx to meet you. He wouldn't tell me why. Just that it was important that he talk to you."

"I don't know anything about it," I said, shaking my head.

"There'd be no reason for Joey to lie to me about it, and Joey did go to the Onyx. If he hadn't, he might not've been murdered. He must have gone there to see you."

I admitted that it could have been true, adding, "But I've no idea at all why he'd want to see me."

"That gives you a reason to look into the murder, doesn't it? Besides money, I mean."

"Nevertheless, I'll take money. Suppose you give me a hundred in advance?"

She didn't bat an eye reaching into her purse and coming up with five twenties.

I pocketed the bills and told her, "I'm not one of those private investigators who drags out a case just for money. If I hit a dead end, I'll let you know right away."

"I appreciate that, Harry."

"Honesty's the best policy, I always say."

She got up and began putting on her fur. "I've written my address and number on the back of that paper with the strange code on it. You can call me there anythime."

"I'll call you as soon as I have something," I said, getting up and crossing the office to open the door for her. "I'll walk down with you. The stairs're dark and tricky."

"Thank you. You're very kind."

"Well, Gloria, you're a client now, and I am always kind to my clients."

When I put her into a taxi, I noticed that she was not unaware of my interest in her legs as she climbed in. She waved at me as the taxi pulled away, wiggling her fingers like a little girl waving at her daddy as she goes off to school for the first time. Only this little girl was wearing red velvet gloves, and one of the fingers had a ring on it big enough to choke a horse.

Going back up to my office, I was bothered by two things. First, how did Joey Seldes ever land a dame like that for a wife? Second, what the hell did Joey Seldes want to see me about on the night he was blasted off the face of the earth?

I stuffed the things Gloria Seldes had left for me—the note, the gun, the clipping—in my pockets. The Colt felt like a cannon compared to my own pistol, a snub-nosed .38 which I wore in a shoulder holster under my left arm. I never kept evidence in my office when it was portable. I'd rifled too many desks and file drawers in presumably locked and secure offices when I was a cop to trust even the best security, which was not exactly what my fourth-floor walk-up provided.

4

The Diamond Caper

It had snowed four inches the previous day, and not much of it had been shoveled away, making for hard going underfoot as I trudged crosstown to the Forty-second Street home of the *Daily News* to look up my friend Ben Turner, who'd been a denizen of Park Row newspapers for years before landing with the *News* and making the trek uptown when the *News* abandoned its rat-trap home on Newspaper Row for a spanking new headquarters at Forty-second and Second in 1930, causing Ben and other ink-stained drinkers to complain mightily about having to discover new speakeasies to carouse in. Ben and I got to know each other when he was a cub reporter and I was a rookie cop. By the time I had a detective's shield, Ben was a star reporter of crime news, first at the *Daily Mirror,* then the *News,* spirited away from the *Mirror* by a fat salary offered by the *News*'s publisher, Captain Joseph M. Patterson. Ben was almost twice the age of most of the other reporters on the crime beat, a little guy with a bald head, horn-rimmed glasses, an Old Testament nose, and a million-dollar smile, which he bestowed on me as I picked my way across the city room on the seventh floor. "What's up?" he asked, leaning back in his chair with his feet propped against his desk.

"I need to know about the Kipinski diamond heist."

"Three million smackers' worth, they say the guy was carrying. Maybe he was and maybe he wasn't," he said, coming down in his chair. "The only word we have that Kipinski had any dia-

18

monds on him at all was the word of his partner, Herschel Siskowitz."

"Do you think Herschel what's-his-name lied?"

"It's possible Herschel what's-his-name swiped the gems himself and got rid of his partner and made up a story about there being a heist."

"You have any evidence of that?"

"Not a shred."

"Nobody ever found Kipinski?"

"Nope."

"Maybe he skipped with the stones."

"It's possible. Anything's possible. But Kipinski was an old man, been in the diamond district forever, great reputation, regular patron of the synagogue in Brooklyn where he lived, a wife as old as he was who's been brokenhearted ever since he vanished. Not a profile of a man who'd skip. Not a guy to have a broad somewhere or big gambling debts. No, I think he was bumped off by somebody."

"One of the mobs?"

Ben nodded. "Could be. I never heard anything for sure about anything like that on the street, but I don't hear everything. *Winchell* hears *everything!* Ask Winchell. He was always tight with Owney Madden and Dutch Schultz and Waxy Gordon and Arnold Rothstein. Me? I know about the cheap hoods and the ordinary criminals who get caught. If there was a major diamond heist by one of the mobs, Winchell'd hear it sooner than me. Ask some of your old pals in the department."

"The cops are at a dead end themselves apparently."

"Yeah. The case is cold. It's been almost two months."

"You must have heard something since then. Rumors. Talk on the streets."

"I heard a while ago that there was speculation that a pair of guys from the Madden mob had done it. Eddie Two Fingers Molloy and Joe the Dude Dennehy. It was just guessing, though, based on the fact that Two Fingers was found dead in a car near the Boardwalk at Coney Island and that the Dude hasn't been seen in these parts since. The speculation was that Two Fingers and the Dude pulled the diamond robbery, fought over the loot, and Two Fingers wound up dead with the Dude skipping out with the gems. I never bought it, though."

"Why not?"

"The Dude was about to get married. Do you know the Dude? A young guy, very good-looking. He was head over heels in love with a gal lives in Queens. They were supposed to get hitched sometime in January. I've seen the girl, and I don't think the Dude would have left town without her, especially if he had three million in diamonds to finance the honeymoon."

"Maybe he's waiting for things to cool off before he sends for her?"

"She doesn't act like a girl who expects to be whisked to paradise by a boyfriend suddenly rich. She's a wreck with worry over what happened to him."

"What do you think happened to him?"

"I think he was rubbed out just like Two Fingers. I don't think either Two Fingers or the Dude had anything to do with the diamond robbery. I figure those two guys were killed for other reasons, mob reasons. They were Madden guys."

"I haven't read anything about the Kipinski case since it happened. Have you dropped it like the cops have?"

"It hasn't been a story for weeks. Maybe I should heat it up again."

"Do me a favor and don't heat it up for a while, Ben."

"Are you working the case for someone?"

"The wife of a punk named Joey Seldes."

"Shit, I knew that creep. Somebody bumped him a while back."

"New Year's Eve. Couple a days after the Kipinski thing."

"Say, he was a Madden boy, too, just like the others. Interesting."

"Isn't it?"

Ben suddenly shook his head. "Nah. Seldes was a two-bit hanger-on. A three-million-dollar diamond deal was far beyond him."

"Have the cops put Seldes on the ice?"

"Yeah. Who cares about someone bumping a cheap hood like

him? Now, with the big shakeup going on in the police department itself, with heads rolling and indictments forthcoming,
cheap murders in clubs don't get a lot of attention. What do you
think of the new Commissioner?"

"Lew Valentine was always good. He should have been put in
right away by La Guardia instead of fuckin' around with John
O'Ryan, a goddamned military man."

"La Guardia and Valentine had quite a chat. Fiorello says to
Lew, 'If I find a policeman taking as much as a Cremo cigar from
anybody, I'll fire him.' To which Valentine responds, 'This department has no room for crooks. I'll be more quick to punish a
thief in a police uniform than any ordinary thief.' I hear Valentine has put out the word to 'muss up' the hoods. He told the
Mayor, 'I want the gangster to tip his hat to the cop.' " Ben
laughed. "What a pair of balls, hunh?" The smile faded and Ben
added, "Maybe you should think about gettin' back on the force,
Harry. Seems to me Valentine would welcome a man like you
back in the ranks."

With a shrug, I replied, "I'm makin' too much dough being
private."

"Hey, I want a promise from you that if you come up with
anything new on the Kipinski caper I'll be the first to know."

"What? Not give it to Winchell?"

Ben frowned. "You give a story to that warmed-over song and
dance man ahead of me and I'll kick your ass all the way to the
Rockaways and back again."

"Okay, but first I want a favor. I want to look at the back
issues of the *News* on the Kipinski case. Can you fix it for me?"

"Easy." He winked. He yelled to a copy boy, who came running. "See that Mr. MacNeil gets anything he wants."

As it turned out, what I wanted wasn't in the papers. The
News added nothing to what I already knew about the disappearance of Shmuel Kipinski. It was a waste of time. But I had
to try. You always have to try, I always say.

5

On the Town

When I left the *Daily News* offices, it was only six o'clock.

It was too early to be able to do any more looking into who killed Joey Seldes and why. The people Joey knew never came out of doors in the daylight. They emerged after dark, filling up the restaurants, the theaters on Broadway, the former speak-easies on The Street and in the other blocks in the fifties. When most people were going home from work, the people Joey Seldes knew and hung out with were just starting the day.

In the meantime, I was wrapping up a divorce case, so I hopped on the Second Avenue el downtown, then strolled to an address in Greenwich Village. The man my client wanted a divorce from would be in the apartment he rented for a young woman who worked in the chorus of a hit show on Broadway. I expected to find them in bed together and did, so it didn't take much persuading to convince the gentleman to grant his wife's desire for a divorce.

"That would be a lot better than finding your name and this pretty girl's name, too, in a Winchell column. Or maybe Ed Sullivan's. You've both got too much to lose in that kind of cheap publicity, eh?" I gave them both a smile and then added, "You know, the wife wanted me to just come down here and shoot you both, but I don't shoot people. Not at these prices."

I closed the door very politely as I left, then had a good laugh at how scared they had been when I mentioned the possibility of murder. I phoned the distraught wife and assured her her husband would see things her way and my bill would be in the mail.

The money was good. Very good. It was a tawdry business but a profitable living. "Tawdry" was the word my old boss in the police department used when I told him I was going to quit being a cop and go private. "A private dick? You?" he scoffed. "You're not cut out of that kind of cloth, Harry."

"A man's gotta eat," I said with a shrug.

"Then stay on the force. Don't quit."

"I'm quitting, Bill. That's decided. I've had enough of the bullshit."

"We need good cops like you, Harry. Hell, you're one of Mayor Walker's favorite cops. He's told me so himself. Jimmy's a friend. He could get you out of this scrape."

"Jimmy's got his own scrapes to get out of."

"Well, if your mind's set, I'll make sure that you don't have any trouble getting licensed and the like."

"Appreciate it, Bill," I said, giving him my hand.

A couple of months after I quit the force and had my license and opened my office, my old captain in the department was indicted. The papers made a big deal of it. Cops on the take had suddenly become big news, even though the whole damned city knew that the cops took payoffs long before the Seabury investigation started making a big splash. "You got off the force just in time," a pal said to me when he read about the latest indictments.

"I didn't have to worry about that crap," I said. "I never was on the take."

And I never was.

I took the Lexington Avenue subway uptown from Astor Place to Grand Central with plans on walking up Fifth Avenue to The Street, but when I arrived at Forty-second and Fifth there was a tussle going on between the cops and a gang of toughs from the German-American Bund. Fists and nightsticks were flying thick and fast on the corner by the library. The cops were outnumbered, but I heard the sirens of paddy wagons and patrol cars coming in all directions, so the balance of power was about to see a shift in favor of the cops. Meanwhile, the boys in khaki shirts with the red-white-and-black armbands were taking a pasting from the sticks in the hands of the cops. A large crowd of on-lookers had gathered on each corner, and traffic was at a stand-still on the streets.

"What started all this?" I asked one of the bystanders, a fat man in an overcoat.

"Those Nazis jumped a Jew kid coming out of the library," the fat man replied.

"What did the kid do?"

"Nothing. He was coming down the steps and those boys were passing by. They jumped him."

Additional cops arrived, and the tide swung decidedly against the Nazis. In a few minutes the boys in blue were pushing the boys in brown into paddy wagons. To the fat man, I said, "We ought to do that to the real Nazis over in Germany."

The fat man shook his head. "Not our business, buddy." He hurried away, turning up the collar of his overcoat, and didn't look back.

Presently, the paddy wagons rattled away with their passengers and Fifth Avenue resumed its usual tranquillity.

From Forty-second and Fifth I hiked over to Times Square, a blaze of light and motion and excitement as dozens of cabs and cars and limos funneled into the world's most famous intersection. The wind was coming hard off the river along Forty-second, and I walked with my head down against it, getting a break only when I turned and started up Broadway with the buildings block-ing the west wind.

If there was a Depression, you couldn't have known it from Broadway that night. It was only Thursday, but the crowds you usually saw only on weekends were already jammed into the streets in and around Times Square. The signs were going and car horns were honking like crazy. Maybe it was the snowstorm the previous day, maybe it was just that people wanted to hurry up and say goodbye to a bleak February and to welcome March, which meant spring was coming, but the crowd was happy along Broadway.

At Forty-fourth Street I ran into Richard Harrison, who was scurrying along on his way to his theater just down the block where he was appearing in *The Green Pastures*. We exchanged hellos, and he hurried on. I knew Harrison from The Street, where he came after his show for the jazz, as so many of the Broadway actors did. Just a few nights before, a gal from the Cole Porter show, *Anything Goes*, had looked in at the Onyx. Everybody on Broadway was saying that Ethel Merman was sensational in the show. She had a mouth and a voice that you could hear on the street outside the Alvin, they said.

It was a great season for Broadway. Bert Lahr and Ray Bolger were in *Life Begins at 8:40* at the Wintergarden as I headed up that way. In the side streets were Kate Cornell in her 690th performance in *The Barretts of Wimpole Street* at the Martin Beck, Tallulah Bankhead at the Music Box in *Rain*, and Leslie Howard in Robert Sherwood's *The Petrified Forest*, with the tough gangster named Duke Mantee being played by a relative newcomer to Broadway with the ungangsterlike name of Humphrey Bogart. A lot of the mobsters who came into the Onyx had heard about Bogart's tough guy and talked about going over to see him personally to see just how rough he was, although none ever did, as far as I knew.

I was half frozen from the cold when I turned off Seventh Avenue to walk the block to the Onyx. When I came in, there was a half-drunk dame talking to trombonist Mike Riley and saying in a singsong boozy voice as she pointed at a French horn Mike was holding, "It must be a very hard instrument to play."

"Not at all." Mike smiled, holding up the horn. "You just blow in here. You push the middle valve down. The music goes round and round, and it comes out here." Trumpeter Ed Farley almost went onto the floor laughing.

I stood at the bar at almost the exact spot where Joey Seldes died. I had a whiskey and then another. The place wasn't filled up yet, it being only a little after eight. Tatum was noodling on the piano, and the joint was quieter than I'd seen it in a long time. Business had picked up since the shooting of Joey had grabbed headlines at the first of the year. A lot of new faces had started coming in, drawn by the notoriety and the expectation of seeing a gangster gunned down every night of the week. Louie said to me, "I heard that Gloria Seldes was up to see you today, Harry."

"She was," I said with a noncommittal voice. I was used to everyone at the Onyx knowing my business. Most of the time I counted on it.

"I guess she's getting back into circulation finally," Louie said.

"I can't figure out what got Gloria Seldes to marry a weasel like Joey," I said, frowning down at my glass.

Louie chuckled. "His schlong."

"What?" I grinned.

"His schmuck. His equipment. Big, man."

"Are you telling me Gloria married him because of the size of his . . . ?"

"Gloria was always a dame with an enormous appetite," Louie said, toweling the bar. "Hell, I thought everybody on The Street knew about Joey's dong. I figured you'd know because you're a pal of Pops Whiteman, who happened to have lost a bundle of money in one of the most famous wagers ever made on this here block. You know how talk on this street always gets around to big instruments. I'm not talking about musical instruments. Wilbur Daniels of the Spirits of Rhythm has a rep for having a really long one. Same for Joe Venuti. Well, one night here at the Onyx, Ben Bernie began gabbing about Seldes's equipment. Pops Whiteman was at a nearby table and got into the conversation. Soon they had a bet going. Next thing you know, Joey comes in and has a few drinks and then goes for the men's room. They took off after him. Nobody said anything to Joey. They just looked. Afterward Whiteman turned to Ben Bernie and paid off without a word."

"Gloria's hired me to check into the shooting. She says she wants to get even with whoever bumped him off. That's what you call wifely loyalty."

"What's her real angle, I wonder?" Louie was always very cynical about things like people's motivations, which is probably why he was a good bartender, understanding people the way he did.

"I've got to talk to some of the people who were here that

night, Louie. You were tending bar. Which of the regulars were around who saw what happened?"

"Well, it was New Year's Eve, and I wasn't exactly counting the house, Harry. But, let's see. Winchell was here when it happened. I'm sure of that. You always know when Winchell's in the joint. Whiteman was in, but I don't know if he was here when the guns went off. The band was here, of course, but they were jamming and didn't even know it had happened until Grady came in with his cops. There was the kid Joey came in with. Don't know his name."

"Joey came in with someone?"

"A young guy. A Dago, I think. He had the look of an Italian. Handsome, surly-looking, shifty. Never said anything. He left in a big hurry when the guns started popping. He was gone before the cops arrived."

"Did you ever see the kid before?"

"Nope. And not since. I just don't remember who else was here, Harry."

"Did Joey ask for me that night, Louie?"

"I don't think so, Harry, but I was damned busy, you know?"

"Who'd've considered Joey Seldes worth bumping off?" I said. Shaking my head, I tapped the rim of my glass, and Louie refilled it. "This place always had the best booze in town, even when it was fresh out of the bathtub," I said with a smile. "You sure you never saw that kid who was with Joey any other time, Louie?"

"Not that I recall. I didn't make watching Joey Seldes a specialty. I could have eyes for his wife, though, I have to admit."

"A real looker."

"A Cadillac body if there ever was one on a woman."

"Say, Louie! You sound like you could fall for her."

"She's out of my league. She'd chew me up and spit me out."

With a grin and a wink, I said, "But think of the fun during the chewing part."

"A woman like that's just too much of a woman to stay the private property of any one guy."

Interested, I asked, "Was she catting around on Joey?"

Louie gave his bartender's shrug, an admission that what he was thinking was more gut feeling than hard evidence. A hunch. Bartenders are like cops when it comes to hunches. Louie did not venture beyond the shrug, and I let it go. I finished my drink, turned, and walked out.

I wanted to look up Winchell and figured he'd be at Hanson's.

6

Gossip

Winchell looked exactly right, as if a tuxedo was what everybody wore when having a sandwich at Hanson's Drug Store at the corner of Seventh and Fifty-first. The place was crowded when I went in. Winchell was at one of the tables in the back, alone, nibbling at his sandwich and looking at his watch as if he were late for a Broadway opening. I pushed past the L-shaped counter toward the tables. A knot of people was gathered around Art Tatum, who tickled the ivories during intermissions in the lounge upstairs at the Onyx but who, now that the band was on, was taking a break for a bite to eat. Fat, jolly, black, incredibly gifted, Tatum was almost totally blind and was doing a trick of his at the counter. Someone would drop a handful of coins on the marble top, and he would tell what coins had plunked down just from the sound of them.

As I slid into a chair at Winchell's table, he gave me the eye, that look of his that was half suspicious, half wondering—suspicious that you were there to try to get something out of him, wondering what he could get out of you for his column. "Harry," he said with a nod, "how's the gumshoe business?"

"Slow," I said. "How's the gossip business?"

"You can read it in the *Daily Mirror*." He flashed a smile.

I smiled back, although I thought he was a prick, always was, and always would be. "Walter," I said, as if I didn't think he was a prick, "you were at the Onyx the night that Joey Seldes was rubbed out?"

29

"Quite a night."

"Yeah. You saw what happened?"

"I'm a reporter, Harry. I see most everything."

"Two guys came in, walked up to Joey, and pumped him full of bullets? That's it?"

"Yes, except for what one of them said."

"One of the gunmen said something to Joey?"

"He said, 'You were told to stay away from the kid.' Then they cut Joey down."

" 'You were told to stay away from the kid.' "

"That's what he said."

"Louie the bartender at the Onyx says there was a kid with Joey that night. The same kid, I wonder?"

"I couldn't say. I didn't see anybody with Joey. I was at the bar, just a couple of people away."

"But you heard the comment about Joey being warned to stay away from a kid?"

"I go to bars to listen, Harry. That's an exact quote."

"You have no idea who the kid was?"

"None, although lately Seldes had been hanging around with a new crowd. I saw him over at the Rainbow Room not long before he was bumped off. He was with some young men that night. They looked like young hoods, possibly from the Luciano mob."

"What makes you say that?"

"One of them was a brother of a guy in the Luciano mob. A hood named Dacapua. The young kid isn't connected. I believe his brother's trying to keep him out of the mobs, although I hear the kid's just the kind of wise guy who'd want in. Anyway, they were having quite a party and wound up giving a hard time to one of the busboys."

"Why were they doing that?"

"I was on my way out and didn't pay that much attention. It wasn't exactly an item, you know? I think the maitre d' stepped in and gave them the heave-ho. Say, what's cooking? Why this interest in Seldes?"

"Walter, how about a little *quid pro quo?*"

"Harry! I'd no idea you were a Latin scholar!"

"I'm a product of a good Catholic education. How about it? You give me a little info and I give you an item?"

"I'll have to hear your *quid* before I make up my mind about any *quo*."

"Do you still have a hard-on for the Nazis?"

"Hate the scummy bastards with a passion, you know that."

"A bunch of 'em took a shellacking down by the library this afternoon at the hands of New York's Finest. You can call downtown and get the particulars. Now for my *quo*. At the Onyx the night Joey got bumped? Did he ask for me?"

"Not with me, he didn't. I didn't hear everything that was said. He could have asked for you. I just don't know," Winchell replied with a shrug. Then he smiled. "The Ratzis took a pasting, hunh?" Since 1933, Walter'd been calling the Nazis "Ratzis" in print.

"Their blood ran in the gutters."

"That's where they belong. Guttersnipes every one."

"My *quo* has a second part, Walter," I said, smiling.

"Ask, already." He sighed.

"The Kipinski diamond heist."

"Ancient history."

"Was it Madden's boys?"

"One of 'em got bumped off, another is among the missing. Some people add it up and come up with the Kipinski thing."

"Do you?"

"It's possible."

"I hear that the two guys involved, Joe the Dude and the other one . . ."

"Eddie Molloy."

". . . might have been free-lancing."

"A dangerous game if Owney finds out."

"Maybe Owney found out and settled their ashes?"

"Owney's been down south."

"Owney has a long arm."

"It's possible."

"But you haven't heard anything in that direction?"

"Nope."

"Thanks, Walter."

"How's this tie in with Seldes?"

"Who said it ties in with Seldes?"

"It smells that way."

"That's why you're such a red hot gossip columnist, Walter. You have a talent to take two and two and make it add up to five."

Winchell's hard blue eyes danced with pleasure. "How'd it be if I put an item in the column something like this: 'One of Gotham's famous private dicks thinks the rubout of a cheap hood and a recent diamond theft have a common denominator'?" He grinned as he said it while under the table his heel was beating the floor like a jazz musician's. "How'd that be, Harry?"

"It'd be wrong, Walter. Like most of the stuff in your column."

Winchell laughed. "I love ya, Harry. I really do. Don't worry. I won't print anything. Thanks for the Ratzi tip."

"Forget it, Walter. See ya."

"Harry!" he called as I headed for the door, "a word of advice! Never forgive an enemy or forget a friend!"

"Which are you, Walter?" I asked.

With a wink, he said, "I'll never tell!"

Outside, despite the freezing wind, I decided to walk over to the RCA Building to follow up on what Winchell had witnessed between Seldes and the busboy at the Rainbow Room. I figured I could use the exercise and maybe the wind would get the smell of Winchell out of my nose.

First I stopped at the Onyx to see if anybody'd left any messages for me at the bar. There were no messages, but Ben Turner was there nursing a scotch and ogling a couple of dames in a booth near the piano. His interest in the women ended when he saw me come in. "You're a man of disgustingly predictable habits, Harry."

"What brings you around here, Ben?"

"I was thinking about your visit to my office and the Kipinski thing. I know you long enough to know that you're onto something that could spell a story for me and my paper. What Charlie MacArthur and Ben Hecht would call a 'scoop.'"

"I'm a long way from anything printable on this, Ben. Maybe it will never be printable."

With a lopsided grin, he replied, "I figure if I keep close tabs on you, you can't slip the story to Winchell."

"I just left him, by the way. Over at Hanson's."

"How can you let yourself be seen in public with that gossip monger?"

"Oh, he can be helpful. You know how it is with reporters, Ben. You never can tell when one of 'em might be worth your time. Besides, you're the one who told me Winchell would have the dope on Owney Madden's activities."

"Did he?"

"Nah."

"Now what?"

"I'm on my way to the Rainbow Room. Want to come?"

"Do they let Jews in?"

"You can turn your collar around and I'll tell them you're my priest."

Ben slid off his bar stool and rubbed his hands together. "I must say, you private dicks know how to live. The Rainbow Room! High society!"

"I hate to disappoint you, Ben, but we're going to the kitchen."

7

Rainbows

From the look of the Rainbow Room, you'd never have known that there were penniless guys selling apples on street corners and plenty of others standing on line in soup kitchens all over town. The rich were out in force, dressed to the nines, eating and dancing in a saloon that had always been too ritzy for my taste, although I'd gone to the Rainbow Room on a few cases and twice just on my own because of the music on the bill. The clear winter night beyond the windows of the sixty-fifth floor of the RCA Building provided a view for miles uptown and down. Manhattan was a black velvet cloth that somebody'd thrown diamonds and rubies on, sparkling like gems on Shmuel Kipinski's jeweler's cloth.

Adoring the splendor beyond the windows, I wondered if I could kill for three million in diamonds and decided that I was capable of anything that human beings do. Had I been presented with a chance to rob and kill Shmuel Kipinski, I would have been capable of it, no doubt, although I told myself I wouldn't've done it. I was convinced someone had killed the old Jew for his little bag of trinkets, and I was open to the possibility that in some way, as crazy as it sounded, Joey Seldes had had a part in it. Whether a noisy scene involving Joey Seldes and a Rainbow Room busboy had any connection with the Kipinski diamonds, I had no inkling.

The maitre d' seemed relieved to find out that Ben Turner and

I had not come to dine in his room but wanted only to talk with a certain employee of the place.

"Yes, I remember the altercation," said the maitre d', shaking his head in disapproval. "I very nearly mistakenly fired the busboy." He smiled, a fatherly smile, maybe even grandfatherly. The headwaiter was a distinguished gentleman with silver hair and an Old Worldliness that spelled class. "I felt sorry for him, however. He's working his way through college. City College, of course. I realized it wasn't his fault what happened."

"What happened?" I asked.

"A party of young men, a little drunk, I suspect, jostled the boy as they were leaving. I tell myself it was unintentional, but I'm not sure."

"I'd like to speak with the boy," I said.

"This is his night off, I'm afraid."

"Could you tell us where he lives? It's very important." To underscore the importance, I dug out a five-dollar bill.

"Please," said the maitre d', raising a forbidding hand. "His name is Joshua Sloman. Avenue B. I would have to look up the number.

"I'd surely appreciate it." I smiled.

The address, which I insisted be paid for with the fiver and which the maitre d' finally accepted, was just around the corner from Houston, a cold-water walk-up railroad-flat tenement in the kind of neighborhood Ben Turner knew well. "I grew up two blocks from here," he announced as we turned from Houston into Avenue B, the two of us bundled against the cold night, which had left the streets nearly empty. I'd never been to the lower east side in the cold, only in the summer, when all the windows were always crowded with women hanging out of them gossiping, yelling down to the pushcart peddlers, or scolding the kids playing in the street.

"You probably know some people on this block," I said to Ben as we searched for the number where Joshua Sloman lived.

"Nah! I was two blocks over. A different street. Different block. Different neighborhood. Different world. You didn't go off

your block. What for? There was trouble enough on your own
street. Here's the Sloman address, Harry."

The Slomans were on the first floor at the back, where the
mother of the family let us in, impressed with my private investigator's card. Her son, Joshua Sloman, a wiry, cautious, cool-eyed,
and worldly youth of, I guessed, eighteen years, was not so impressed. Merely curious. "You came all the way down here just
to ask me about a nothing argument with a bunch of drunks
weeks ago where I work?"

"Did you know those guys?" I asked.

"Never saw them before, but I know their type. Mr. Turner
knows the type, too. Jew baiters."

"The row in the Rainbow Room was because you're Jewish?"
I had my doubts, and they were hardly concealed.

"That's what it was. Four or five of those punks, drunk,
mouthing off. Their leader gave me a shove and said that an ugly
Jew-boy ought to get out of the way of respectable paying customers who happen to be the Jew-boy's betters."

"Did you ever see that guy before?"

"No. I'd've remembered, because he was a little shrimp acting
like a big fish. Showing off for his pals. Loud mouth. He was a
genuine gold-plated schmuck." He whispered the last word so his
mother couldn't hear it.

"Did you know any of the others?"

"I'd never seen any of them."

"Could one of them have been an Italian?"

"All goys look alike to me. Especially when they've got tuxedos
on. Sorry. Nothing personal. I shouldn't make racial slurs, I
know." He glanced at his mother apologetically, then back at me.
"What's so important about those creeps, anyway?"

"One of them may be connected with a murder investigation
I'm conducting."

"I wouldn't be surprised at all to learn he was a killer."

"In this case, he was the victim. If it's the same guy."

"I'd recognize the ones who were with him, in case you have
pictures or something like that."

"No such luck. It may not be connected at all. It's a long shot."

Outside, Ben Turner hunched up his shoulders against the cold, tugged at the brim of his hat, and blew steam from his mouth. "It happened to me once, what happened to Joshua that night."

"What?" I asked, turning toward Houston Street.

"Jew baiting. On my first assignment as a reporter, some of the reporters on that beat made an issue of me being Jewish. You'd think reporters would be more liberal than that, hunh? Ha! I had to kick a few asses." He grunted, gave the pavement a kick, blew a little more steam, and looked at me sidewise. "The incident involving young Joshua's a dead end, I guess?"

"I learned a little. Not much, though."

"I understand how it is. What you do and what I do for a living are alike. We prospect for gold by digging around for little bits of ore—a bit of color here, a bit there, a scrap from over there. Then we have to put it all together like a mosaic. No, more like a rainbow! Yeah. A rainbow of facts, and we hope at the end of the rainbow'll be the pot of gold—truth. For me, a good story in the paper. For you, a solved case and a happy client."

"Right, Ben. Poetic and right."

"Let's get a taxi, Harry. I'm freezing my gonads off."

In the cab, Ben was silent, thoughtful, until a couple of blocks later when he said, "These days it seems if you want to show how tough you are you just pick out the nearest Jew-boy and pummel him. I don't wish anybody to be murdered, but I'm not exactly lamenting the passing of Joey Seldes if all he could think of to impress his young friends was rough up a busboy."

"I'm no closer to finding out the name of the kid who was with Joey that night at the Onyx. The way he got the hell out of there, according to Louie, I figured he must have known the killers. Or, at the very least, knew why they'd come in to get Joey."

"I wonder why they didn't kill the kid, too?"

"Winchell said he heard one of the gunmen say to Joey, 'You were told to stay away from the kid.' The kid Joey was supposed to stay away from was probably the kid he was with. Make sense?"

"Yeah. If you can believe Winchell."

"I believe him, Ben."

As the rumpled reporter stared out the window at passing real estate, it wasn't hard to imagine wheels turning in his inquisitive mind digging for bits of color to make a rainbow. He looked back at me at last. "Would you mind if I look over your shoulder on this thing, Harry? If you don't want me meddling, say so."

"Hey! You're a reporter. You've got a right."

"I was thinking, maybe we could turn up something if we had a talk with that gal over in Queens who was hoping to marry Joe the Dude. She might have some idea if the Dude and Joey Seldes were thick."

"You keep coming back to the Kipinski diamonds the way I do when I try to puzzle this out."

"Three million in ice could make a guy who always wanted to be a big shot start acting like one in earnest."

"We'll see the lady in Queens, Ben, soon."

"What now?"

"There was one other person at the Onyx who might have seen the kid Joey was with and might know who the kid is. Pops Whiteman."

"Is that where you're going now?"

"Well, Whiteman could be in any one of a hundred gin joints in this town at this hour. I'll just have to look around for him. Wanna come?"

"You can drop me at home. I'm in no condition to go saloon crawling at my age."

"Do you mean to say you aren't the man you used to be, Ben?"

"None of us is, Harry. That's the godawful truth."

I left Ben at his apartment house near New York University and began searching all over town for the corpulent, brilliant, fun-loving "King of Jazz"—Paul Pops Whiteman. He was not at any of the joints I visited and it wasn't until the last one that I was told that in all likelihood I'd find Pops tomorrow afternoon at a certain address at 103rd and Riverside.

8

Pops

My taxi was slow getting up Riverside Drive because huge
trucks were hauling stone to a project where the city was widen-
ing Riverside Park, but soon I was on the pavement outside the
house where, if you didn't know who lived there, you could guess
from the music spilling out the windows. I recognized a tune from
Oh, Kay, George Gershwin's 1926 hit show, and when I was let
into the Gershwin apartment, the composer was at the piano
caressing the keys to fill the room with "Someone to Watch Over
Me." There appeared to be a party going on, with all the guests
gathered around Gershwin. In their midst wast he unmistakable
figure of the man I'd come to see.

Whiteman broke away from the crowd when Gershwin finished.
As the guests applauded, Pops charged over to me and threw his
arms around me in an embrace. He gave real meaning to the expression "bear hug." He was as big as a grizzly. Biggest man I
ever knew. "Harry! How the hell are you?" He laughed and
patted my belly. "You're getting a pot, Harry. Watch out or
you'll be buying your suits from my tailor. I heard you were
looking for me last night. I was going to ring you up today. Now
I don't have to! Glad you're here. There's a real treat coming
up that an appreciator of great music such as yourself will really
want to hear."

The treat was Gershwin at the piano playing music from a new
work he was close to completing, an opera, no less, called *Porgy*

and Bess, which Gershwin was collaborating on with a writer named Dubose Heyward, who lived in South Carolina. They'd been working through the mail, an achievement which boggled my mind. At the piano, Gershwin began "Summertime," from his opera in progress, and Pops and I fell silent, something both he and I were bound to do in the presence of fine music.

Pops Whiteman was the first truly famous person I had ever met, although there'd been quite a few criminals and otherwise notorious persons in my acquaintance prior to February 12, 1924, the date on which I met Whiteman at Aeolian Hall. He was thirty-four years old at the time and had just stood New York on its ear by announcing that he was going to present an all-jazz concert—he called it "An Experiment in Modern Music"—featuring new compositions by Irving Berlin, Victor Herbert, and George Gershwin, who, Whiteman boasted, was composing a jazz concerto especially for the Aeolian Hall event. As it turned out, Gershwin had been at work on no such thing, but having been publicly committed to a new work, he came through—not with a concerto but a composition he called an American rhapsody and which his brother Ira named *Rhapsody in Blue*. At that time, I was a beat cop usually drafted for duty at public events such as important funerals, the St. Patrick's Day parade, and boxing at Madison Square Garden. For the Aeolian Hall concert, I volunteered, wangling a post inside the hall.

The place was packed and electric with anticipation, but by the time the program reached the Gershwin, the audience had had to sit through at least twenty numbers. They were, to say the least, fidgety as Gershwin took his place at the piano. Whiteman dominated the podium. Then came a clarinet glissando by Ross Gorman that quieted the hall as surely as if someone had flipped a switch. For me, a rank amateur on the licorice stick, that opening glissando was a revelation. Never mind that it was one of the most famous musical openings ever.

After the concert, I rushed backstage and grabbed Whiteman by the arms so strongly he must have thought he was being arrested. Amused and delighted to hear such praise pouring off the lips of a lowly uniformed cop, Whiteman gleefully introduced me to Ross Gorman and then to the composer of *Rhapsody in Blue*. Between the Aeolian triumph and our later regular encounters at the Onyx, Pops Whiteman had gone on to be known as "The King of Jazz," thanks to his championing of the cause of jazz and due in no small measure also to his role in a movie in 1930 which happened to be titled "The King of Jazz." His was one of two large pictures hanging on the wall at the Onyx. The other was of Mildred Bailey. I saw Gershwin less often than Pops, but when I did, it was always as thrilling as that first time in 1924.

The last haunting notes of "Summertime" were shimmering in Gershwin's apartment like humidity in the air just before an August thunderstorm as Pops roused himself from the spell of the music to clap me on the shoulder and ask, "What brings you uptown, Harry?"

"I was hoping you could be of help to me on a case."

"Glad to, although I'm mystified."

"You were at the Onyx the night they killed Joey Seldes?"

"I sure was. Quite a thing."

"Did you witness it?"

"No, but I heard it."

"By any chance did you notice if there was anyone with Joey, besides the gunsels who blasted him, I mean?"

Pops reflected a moment, then nodded his head, setting his great flabby jowls rippling. "There was a young fellow with him. I remember thinking that the kid had to be under age and what a stink Joe Helbock would raise if he found out."

"Did you know who the kid was?"

"Sorry. But I'd seen him *before!* At the Cotton Club." He was about to go on, but his attention was distracted by the approach of our host.

Gershwin was smiling as he came our way. The smile was the nicest thing about a face which just missed having the right proportions to be called ruggedly handsome, as if the cosmic recipe for masculine good looks had gone awry. The facial bones were large and raw, the nose had been broken, the chin was almost Neanderthal in its bulkiness, the lower lip curled down and made him look as if he were sneering if he wasn't smiling. The eyes, however, were playfully bright and alert, soaking up everything, absorbing feelings and impressions that would pour out in his music. "How'd you like the number, Harry?" he asked.

"There's no such thing as a bad Gershwin tune, Mr. Gershwin," I replied.

"When are you going to start calling me George like everyone else?"

"I'm looking forward to *Porgy and Bess,*" I said.

"We'll open in Boston in the autumn. *If* I finish it. I'll see that you get tickets when we come to New York, Harry."

"That'd be fine." I beamed.

He excused himself and drifted toward his milling guests. They swallowed him up and drenched him with praise, and I thought he didn't look or act at all like someone that famous and that great.

Whiteman was tugging at my sleeve. "What about the Seldes murder?" He pushed and pulled me to a table loaded with all kinds of booze and then over to a couch where he promptly ignored his gin. "I want all the particulars."

He listened with unblinking fascination, as rapt by my tale of murder as he had been by the sultry melodies by Gershwin. I concluded the story by telling him, "Since Joey apparently walked into that ambush on his way to see me, I'm kind of obligated to get to the bottom of the killing. Even without having been hired, I'd feel that way, once I knew Joey'd come looking for me."

"Surely you're not blaming yourself?" asked Pops, patting my knee.

"Nah, but it gets to me, not knowing what Joey'd wanted and how maybe if I'd been there he wouldn't've been killed."

"They would have killed him somewhere else." Pops sighed with sad, absolute certainty. "Do you believe he was mixed up in the diamond robbery?"

"It's out of character, but it's beginning to look that way."

"And this young man who was with him?"

"He may be able to tell me something to make this puzzle make sense."

"He's a key to the lock!"

"Key or not, he's my only lead."

"Yes, I see that."

"Can you be of any help, Pops?"

"No, afraid not, except to recall— Yes, I'm sure! I am very sure that our mutual friend Sliphorn Kelly knows the kid. Slip and Joey and the mysterious young man were very chummy that night at the Cotton Club. I remember very clearly seeing Joey and Slip having what looked like a damned serious discussion by the bandstand. Slip was sitting in that night for the regular trombonist; and while the band was taking five, Slip and Joey had a long conversation over in a corner. The young man stood nearby, although I don't recall him actually talking to Sliphorn. I had a distinct feeling that the young man was very uneasy about having anything to do with a member of the band at the Cotton Club. He looked like someone who didn't mind going up to Harlem for booze and jazz but who wouldn't feel right about openly being friendly with Negroes."

"Is Sliphorn still working at the Cotton?"

Pops shrugged, his great shoulders shifting like a pair of mountain ridges suddenly jolted into motion by a deep convulsion by the earth's crust. "I haven't seen Sliphorn since that night. You know how he is."

"Off on a toot, you think?"

"As I say, you know how Sliphorn is."

"I do. Thanks for your help."

As I got up to go, Pops seemed surprised. "Leaving? George is just warming up! Plenty of great Gershwin tunes yet to be heard this afternoon."

It was a temptation, but business came first. "You know how I am when I'm on a case, Pops."

"Sliphorn has his kind of dope, you have yours." Whiteman sighed.

"Everybody's got a vice of some kind, Pops. Sliphorn has dope. I've got my work."

"Of all addictions, Harry, yours is the worst." Pops laughed.

With that, I left behind an afternoon of Gershwin.

Going downtown, in the distance I could see floe ice in the Hudson, and it made me think about Shmuel Kipinski, about whether his tied and weighted corpse was mired somewhere in the wintry water of the Hudson or over in the East River, which seemed more likely. There was something about the Hudson that exempted it from the ignominy of being a dumping place for corpses. Its waters were more suited to the berthing of graceful ocean liners at piers at the foot of midtown streets. On the other bank of it, the tree-grown Jersey Palisades shot up from the water, majestic cliffs.

The East River, however, was a working-world river—not a river at all, really—clogged with garbage scows, oil tankers, and rusty freighters that seemed to sneak sheepishly into the harbor through the Narrows and past the Battery, destined for docks in Brooklyn or Long Island or up in the Bronx. Bodies floated often in the East River, where there were more places you could go to dump them without being noticed. I wondered when Shmuel Kipinski's body would float to the top to everyone's astonishment and embarrassment.

I also got to thinking about the curious string of events that connected—if only in my head—two totally different characters by the names of Shmuel Kipinski and Sliphorn Kelly. It was outlandish to consider that a quiet, respectable elderly Jewish gem dealer from Brooklyn could be associated with a character named Sliphorn Kelly, who played jazz trombone and used dope and passed for white when it suited him and by whom no vice had gone untasted. Yet Shmuel Kipinski and Sliphorn Kelly were fox-trotting through my head amid a slew of questions and more unaccounted-for people than in any case I'd ever handled. Where was Shmuel Kipinski? (In the East River, probably.) Where were his diamonds? Who was the Italian kid Joey'd been with? Where was Joe the Dude? And how the hell was I going to track down Sliphorn Kelly if he was off on a toot with one of his exotic narcotics? But the question that kept pushing aside all the others was How did a tinhorn like Joey Seldes fit into the tangled web of people and events bedeviling me while the meter clicked off the nickels as the cab barreled down Broadway?

The taxi swung off the Great White Way at Fifty-second and deposited me at the Onyx door. I was inside only about ten minutes, nursing a scotch, when Louie answered the phone behind the bar and handed the receiver to me, whispering, "It's *her*."

She murmured through the phone as if she had her lips next to my ear in bed, or as if she didn't want someone else on her end to hear. "I was hoping I'd find you there. I've been calling your office all day."

"I'm not there much," I said, fishing a Lucky from my pack on the bar. Louie lit me, grinning lewdly. Through smoke, I said into the phone, "I don't have anything to report. It's early. I've had a few leads. Not much. You want to call it off? I'll be into a third day soon."

"I don't want you to call it off."

"That's good." I didn't tell her that there was no way now that I'd call it off, even if she stopped bankrolling me, with me knowing that Joey had been looking for me that night and thinking maybe it was his looking for me that drew him to the Onyx and death. "What did you call about?" I asked her.

"Can you come over?" she whispered.

"Come over? To your place?" I looked at Louie, who was almost on the floor laughing. "I could be there in half an hour," I told her. She hung up and I handed Louie the phone. "Don't say nothing, Louie!"

"I guess her days get lonely now, hm?" he said anyway as I wheeled off the stool and out the door.

She was all in red again, dressed to the nines, when I arrived. She gave me a scotch and then asked me to take her out on the town.

Gloria Seldes was quite a woman. She drank Cointreau sidecars and smoked Marlboros, a woman's cigarette with ivory tips, and she went in for hats that tilted to the right. She wore scarves and dresses that were Fifth Avenue dear and accented her shape, which she told me she maintained by avoiding sweets, although she loved Whitman's chocolates, which Joey always bought her and she always threw away the minute he wasn't looking. She laughed at that in a throaty way that went along with her Cointreau sidecars and her peekaboo hat.

She passed up the pastry tray after we'd had dinner at the

English Grill in the Commodore Hotel, where the music was by
the Johnny Johnson band. Our table talk was small talk. Neither
one of us mentioned Joey. We weren't at all like a detective and
his client. We might have been an ordinary guy and his girl on
a date. I was trying to figure out what she was up to, why she'd
called me. I decided to let her bring up the subject in her own
time. Besides, I was enjoying the music and looking forward to
the vocalist, Violet Rita Mele, but when she was introduced,
Gloria Seldes announced that she wanted to leave. I was deter-
mined to play along with her, and not just because she was
my client. I had a feeling something really personal was bothering her, something she probably thought I could help her out
with.

Suddenly she started working up to it, saying, "You probably
think badly of me, going out like this, calling you up and asking
you to come over, and then asking you to take me out on the
town? You probably are thinking that I ought to behave more
like a woman who's just lost her husband."

"That was weeks ago. I never gave it a thought. I don't hold
to long periods of mourning. I don't make judgments."

She put her hand on my arm and looked at me with very sad
eyes. "I've been lonely, Harry, and since you were a friend of
Joey's—"

"Hold it, Gloria. I wasn't Joey's friend."

"He thought you were. He was on his way to see you when ..."

I shook my head. "I haven't been able to find anyone who can
vouch for that."

"As God is my witness, Harry, it's true."

She sounded deeply hurt and seemed about ready for tears, so
my words came out gentle, if not true. "I know Joey wouldn't
have lied to you. He told you he was coming to see me. He must
have been."

"You don't have to believe me if you don't want to."

"Look, I believe you. If not for you, I wouldn't have started
digging into this case. It was you who told me about Joey coming
to look for me at the Onyx. As you said, that makes it personal.
Of course, you're still paying me."

"Whatever it takes, Harry. All I've got."

Violet Rita Mele began torching "All Through the Night" from the Cole Porter hit over at the Alvin.

"Let's leave, Harry. Okay?" pleaded Gloria. "I hate girl singers."

In the back of the taxi she sat close to me and made no effort to pull away her hand when I lifted it in mine. I thought if I held her hand she'd feel better. Suddenly, she was all over me, kissing me on the mouth and running her hands over my chest. "It's been a long time, Harry," she murmured. "Joey would understand. Joey would—"

"Never mind Joey for now." I kissed her hard.

Later, in bed, she giggled and asked, "Does the time we just had go on my bill?"

"Nah. I turned off the meter an hour ago."

She laughed and rocked the bed, then lit a Marlboro while I smoked a Lucky. After a while, she turned serious and asked me about the case like a client would if we were in my office. I told her what I knew and explained that it might not seem like much, because I was just starting. "The kid Joey was with that night is the key. I'm hoping Sliphorn Kelly can tell me who the kid was. You have no idea?"

"I never knew half the people Joey knew, and didn't want to."

"You never saw Joey with a young Italian kid?"

"Never," she said firmly. She reached for an ashtray by my side of the bed to put out her cigarette, and as she moved, her breasts scraped against my chest. I reached up and pulled her mouth down to mine. We kissed, and the next thing I knew it was two in the morning and I was reaching for my pants to leave.

She was surprised, to say the least. "What is there to do at two in the morning that's better'n this?"

"Finding Sliphorn Kelly, I hope," I said.

Her new apartment was on East Fifty-sixth just over from Second, a one-bedroom on the first floor, and not all that long a walk from the Onyx, so I hiked it, feeling sorry on the way about

lonely Gloria Seldes and hoping I'd made her feel better. I cov
ered the distance in about fifteen minutes, turning off Fifth into
Fifty-second to observe, much to my amazement, a supercharged
Auburn speedster parked outside 21. There was only one car like
that that I knew of that would be parked at that hour right in
front of 21.

Owney Madden was back in town.

9

Owney the Killer

A newspaper guy once wrote that Owney Madden was a little banty rooster out of hell. Owney took no offense. In fact, he was flattered. Had Owney been offended, the reporter would have been dragged from the East River one morning. Owney was no one to mess around with, offend, or doublecross; and if he wiggled a finger at you, you were wise to go and see what he wanted. Owney began wiggling a finger at me as soon as he saw me come into the club. He patted the cushion of the seat next to him as he asked, "How's the Mick Dick?"

"Great, Mr. Madden," I replied, sitting beside him.

He opened a pack of Spud menthol cigarettes and offered me one, but I said I preferred Luckies. I didn't tell Owney that I'd made up my mind never to smoke anything that sounded as if it had been made from potatoes. Owney talked through Spud smoke. "Whatcha workin' on, Harry?"

I stared down at the tablecloth and smoothed out a wrinkle with my palm before I looked up with a smile and replied, "You tell me what you're working on and I'll tell you what I'm working on, Mr. Madden."

The little gangster coughed a laugh. "As tight-lipped as ever, hunh?"

"In my business, you gotta keep a tight lip," I said, looking at him.

He nodded. "I understand. You and me are in professions with many secrets."

"It's not that I go around collecting secrets. I just don't advertise my business."

"I never saw the value of advertising either." Madden smiled, his brows arching up, his eyes crinkling with his little joke about his line of business. "On the other hand, I've always found it a good policy to know a lot about a lot of things."

"Including other people's business."

"Especially"—he laughed—"other people's business. I hear tell that you've got yourself quite a new client."

"You're referring to Gloria Seldes?"

"Yeah."

"That's no secret. Everybody at the Onyx knew the day she walked in."

"It was a terrible thing, what happened to Joey. I knew him, casually. A lot of people thought he worked for me. People have this idea that I have some kind of organization that people work for. I'm just a happy-go-lucky guy living in semi-retirement. That's neither here nor there. I was talking about Joey Seldes. Sad thing, him being gunned down like that. I sent him a very large spray of flowers to the funeral. It seemed an appropriate gesture, even though I didn't know Joey that well."

"They say Joey had ideas about moving up in the world."

"I've heard that, too. What else have you heard?"

"Joey might have hit onto something really big, they say."

"I heard that, too. Something about some lost property?"

"Something like that."

Madden flicked an ash from his Spud and sipped from a tall glass of mineral water. As he put the water down, he ran the tip of his finger around the rim of the glass. "I'm laying off the booze. I drink mineral water. Been having digestive upsets. Been under a lot of pressure."

I thought about La Guardia and Lew Valentine and smiled inwardly, but outwardly I frowned in sympathy and told Madden I was sorry to hear he wasn't feeling well. "You're alive, though, and that's what counts, I always say."

"Not like Joey Seldes, who's dead." Madden shrugged.

"Along with Two Fingers Molloy."

Madden nodded. "Strange, ain't it, that two guys who were supposed to have been in my employ are dead?"

"And a third missing."

Madden sipped his mineral water thoughtfully, then asked, "Is someone missing?"

"The word around town is that Joe the Dude Dennehy walked out on a wedding planned for last month."

"I assume he got cold feet. It's crazy! A man gets hot pants for a dame, and as often as not the hots turn into a bad case of cold feet."

"A very philosophical observation, Mr. Madden."

"When you're in semi-retirement, you get to think a lot, and philosophize, and read. For instance, did you ever hear of a man named Dr. Russell Conwell?"

"Nope."

"He founded a college down in Philly and had this outlook on life which he called 'Acres of Diamonds.'"

"Ah! Acres of diamonds! That'd be a sight for tired eyes."

"Yeah, it sure would."

"I don't suppose this Conwell guy was talking about real diamonds? I mean, he was probably being philosophical, hypothetical."

"Like you and me right now. We're not talking about real diamonds either. We're in an area of gems of thought, so to speak." Madden coughed another laugh. "Yeah, gems of thought!"

"That's fine, Mr. Madden, because if it got around to real diamonds, I wouldn't have much to say."

"No, I guess not, you being a tight-lipped fellow."

"The only diamonds I ever see are behind thick pieces of glass in the windows of shops down in the diamond district. You know, along Forty-seventh Street? I can never afford to buy any, so I just stand outside the windows and peer in."

Madden ground out his Spud and immediately lit another. "That street is very curious. Know much about the diamond district, Harry?"

"About as much as anyone else."

"It's a Jew monopoly, you know. Hassidics. Is that what they call those Jews with the long black coats, those funny black hats, and the long hair? Hassidim, or something like that. They're diamond merchants, practically every one. I've been told that if you pass one of those Yids on the street the chances are very good that he's got a little pile of diamonds right there in his coat pocket, valued maybe couple a hundred thousand."

Nodding, I said, "I seem to recall a newspaper story a few weeks back about one of those diamond merchants who disappeared. The paper said he was carrying stones of three million in value, easy."

"Isn't that amazing?"

"I thought so. Even more amazing, Mr. Madden, is the fact that they've never found the diamond merchant. Nor the diamonds, of course."

"A victim of a crime, no doubt."

"Apparently. There was a rumor that the merchant was waylaid by a couple of hoodlums from one of the city's mobs."

"A rumor is a mischievous thing, Harry."

"I don't want to come off like Walter Winchell, but being a man who works on the streets, I pick up gossip from time to time."

"Naturally."

"Well, there was some talk that the diamond merchant who vanished was kidnapped and disposed of by a couple of mavericks in one of those mobs—two fellows who pulled the job on their own without bothering to tell the mob's boss about it."

Madden clucked his tongue. "Not a healthy thing to do."

"Even fatal."

"Did you hear any other gossip? More recent?"

"Not a thing. How about you?"

"I also heard the theory about a pair of mavericks, as you call them, doing a job without permission; but I don't know what to make of something else I heard."

"What would that be?"

"That the two fellows who pulled this diamond caper on their own could have been victims themselves of a third party, not the boss of the mob they supposedly worked for."

"That's very interesting."

"Ain't it? I thought so. Trouble is, the story that reached me way down there in Arkansas, where I've been these past months, is that the third party may have met an untimely death himself, without telling anyone where the diamonds were stashed."

"It would be a damned lucky thing if someone accidentally came across that stash, wouldn't it?"

"It would be a very big payday."

"Unfortunately, I've never had that kind of luck."

Madden smiled coyly. "What's that jazz I always heard about the luck o' the Irish?"

"Bullshit, mostly."

"Well, St. Patty's Day's not far off. Maybe a little leprechaun will come your way. If one hasn't already."

"I don't know what I'd do if I happened to run into that kind of luck, Mr. Madden."

"Yeah, I see what you mean. I'm just guessing, mind you, but I bet it would be very difficult even for you to unload three million dollars' worth of stolen diamonds, unless . . ."

"Unless I had connections for handling merchandise like that?"

Madden lifted up his hands. "Who has connections like that?"

"Who, indeed?"

"It's been said that *I* have certain connections, and I don't deny that I have a flair for business transactions of a certain stripe."

"A fellow would probably be wise to keep that in mind if he had a stroke of the luck we've been discussing. The only trouble is, I don't have any diamonds, Mr. Madden."

"This doesn't mean you might never have any diamonds."

"True, Mr. Madden."

"I'm staying at the Waldorf during my visit, Harry, in case you ever have need to get in touch with me."

"I'll keep that in mind, Mr. Madden."

"It would be a very good idea, Harry," Madden said. Then he

glanced at his gold pocket watch. "It's late, and it's very cold outside. I've kept my driver waiting a long time out there."

"I noticed your car but I didn't see the driver, Mr. Madden."

The gangster cracked a smile. "I sent him down the street on an errand, but I expect he'll be back by now, waiting for me in the car. Good night, Harry."

10

The Visit

I never had much in the way of furnishings in my office four floors over the Onyx, so there was not much that had to be put back into place after the tossing that Madden's errand boy had given it while I'd been chatting politely with Owney at 21. When I opened my door, flicked on the light, and discovered the mess, I laughed out loud. By having my office ripped apart by his hood, Owney had told me more about himself than he'd found out about me. Obviously, Owney hoped I might have the Kipinski diamonds. At the very least, he figured I was onto their whereabouts. If he was thinking along those lines, he had to have some evidence that Joey Seldes had known a lot about the diamond heist. As hard as it was for me to buy the idea that Joey had played a role in the caper, Owney's attention to me and his interest in my interest in Joey Seldes pointed no other way. Still, the prospect of Joey Seldes connected with a daring three-million-dollar diamond grab was still so preposterous, I had to laugh about it as I uprighted my couch, put the cushions back on it, and lay down for some sleep.

The next morning, I called up Ben Turner, and we met at a greasy-spoon place called the Sandwich Man next to the *Daily News*. Ben had coffee strong enough to remove paint. I had scrambled eggs, toast, and the coffee. Ben slurped his java. (The only thing I found to criticize Ben for, ever, was the noises he made with coffee. He had this belief that hot liquids in cups and bowls were musical instruments.) He alternately slurped and listened as I told him about my chat with Owney and the visit by his flunky. I concluded, "Owney adds it up this way: The Kipinski diamonds were grabbed by Molloy, the Dude and Joey Seldes."

Ben grunted a laugh. "Good old Joey finally made the big time, eh?"

"If Owney believes it, who am I to argue? He's bound to have inside dope on what happened."

"If Madden's right, then it was the Dude and Joey who bumped off Eddie Molloy."

"And I have to consider the probability that the Dude set Joey up that night at the Onyx. He could have hired a couple of torpedoes to gun Joey down."

"Leaving the Dude with three million all to himself!"

"To finance a honeymoon with his doll in Queens."

"Jesus, what a caper," said Ben with a shake of his head. "What a *story!*"

"Do you have time to come along to Queens for a little visit with the Dude's girl friend?"

Clapping on his hat, Ben exclaimed, "Try and stop me!"

Ben wangled a *Daily News* car to take us to the address of Mary Margaret Mulligan in the middle of a row of attached houses on a quiet street near Jamaica Bay, not far from Floyd Bennett Airfield. The slender red-haired freckled young woman remembered Ben from his previous interview of her when he was writing about the murder of Eddie Molloy. He told her I was also a reporter, adding with only a slight twisting of truth, "Mr. Mac-Neil has been working on another news story, also a murder."

"Oh, my," said Mary Margaret Mulligan, pressing a delicate hand to her chest, then toying with a small rope of imitation pearls. "It must be very exciting being newspapermen."

"The victim in the story I'm working on was named Seldes. He may have known your fiancé. Did Joe Dennehy ever mention anyone by the name of Seldes, Miss Mulligan?"

"I don't believe I ever heard the name before, Mr. MacNeil."

"He was a small fellow. Wiry. Not exactly handsome. Wore flashy clothes?"

"No," she said, shaking her head and tossing her beautiful red hair.

"Have you had any news of your boyfriend, Mary?" asked Ben, always one to get to the point, no matter how bluntly.

"I haven't." Mary Margaret Mulligan sighed, giving a little extra twist to her fake pearls while pearls of tears suddenly formed in the corners of her eyes.

"Well," I said, cutting off whatever Ben's next question was going to be, "we're sorry to have bothered you, Miss Mulligan. Thanks for your time."

"Think nothing of it." She smiled. Brushing away the hovering tears, she escorted us to the door.

In the car, as Ben made a U-turn in the narrow street, I said, "She doesn't know a thing about any of this. Obviously, Joe the Dude is not breaking down her door to run away with her to share in his new-found wealth."

"Yeah," admitted Ben grumpily, "the dame's so damned innocent she could pose for a subway poster about Catholic purity."

"She's better off without Joe the Dude, that's for sure. That's for damned sure," I said. I thought, Mary Margaret, you are a lot better off with fake pearls than real diamonds, that's also for damned sure.

"Where to?" Ben asked.

"I think I should have a talk with Kipinski's partner, Herschel what's-his-name."

"Siskowitz," said Ben, handling the *News*'s Ford with all the expertise you'd expect to find in a New York hack driver. "You won't get anything from him. I tried back at the time his partner vanished. Herschel is as tight as a clam."

"Clams open up when you steam them," I replied. "Wanna come along?"

"I'll drop you. I still work for Captain Patterson's scandal sheet, you know."

I got out at Forty-seventh and Fifth. Ben needled his black Ford into traffic, dangerously cutting in front of a Fifth Avenue double-decker bus. It was only a few steps to an arcade where Herschel Siskowitz plied his trade in precious stones. He rented a cubicle with his name and Kipinski's painted on the door. He was far younger than I'd expected—slender, pale, suspicious-eyed, studying me with the shrewd insight of a diamond merchant who knew instinctively that I was not coming in to price an engagement ring for my fiancée. I knew from the look he gave me that he suspected I was a cop, so I was prepared to play it straight with him, showing him my private investigator's identification; but when he asked me if I was an investigator from an insurance company, I told him I was. He got right down to business at that point. "My policy entitles me to full value of my loss."

"We're talking here about a very large sum, Mr. Siskowitz."

"I paid the premiums. I'm entitled. The life insurance firm has already agreed in principle to pay the full amount of Mr. Kipinski's life policy. I do not understand why your firm is being so reticent about the policy on the merchandise."

"Life insurance companies insure people, Mr. Siskowitz. *We* insure *diamonds*."

The merchant blinked narrow brown eyes. Then he cracked a very sly smile. "What a cynical fellow you are!"

"Hard as diamonds." I winked.

"There is nothing out of order about my claim," he announced, our moment of frosty geniality fading like a miler in a mile-and-a-quarter at Belmont.

"Well, Mr. Siskowitz—"

"Pardon me. Ziskowitz. With a Z."

"Ah! With a Z?" Turning and looking at the names backwards on the closed glass door, I read Ziskowitz, the Z looking like an S. "Easy mistake to make," I said, turning back to the black-clad merchant with a frown. "The problem is, although his life insurance company may pay off, there really is no evidence that your partner is actually dead, not to mention the fact that the diamonds are still missing."

Ziskowitz exploded in anger. "I will not listen to insinuations that my partner and I have done something illegal."

"You must understand that we have to consider all the ramifications."

"Leave my store, Mr. MacNeil! I will deal with the insurance company directly in this matter. I will not tolerate accusations."

"I'm not accusing."

"You will next be suggesting I had something to do with the disappearance of my partner."

"*Did* you have anything to do with it?"

"*Get out!*"

"I was thinking that it might be very profitable to arrange to have a partner robbed, collect the insurance, and still have the diamonds to peddle in your little shop here."

"Slander!"

"Is that what happened, Mr. Z?"

"Leave now or I will press the alarm button and summon police."

"I'm going, Mr. Z."

"And don't come back."

"We'll see what I do."

"I will report you to the insurance company."

"Go right ahead." I smiled.

"This is outrageous conduct on your part."

I was at the door, holding it open and studying the names, frontwards. Ziskowitz. With a Z. *Mr. Z is the man to see on 47 when it is safe,* said the curious note Gloria had brought me the day she hired me. "Say, Mr. Z, have you heard from Joey Seldes lately?"

"I don't know who you are talking about. Who is Mr. Seldes? Is he with the insurance company?"

"No"—I laughed, going out—"he's not with any insurance company."

At the corner, I used a pay phone to call Ben Turner. "That was fast. What did Siskowitz have to say?" he asked.

"I thought you were a hotshot reporter, Ben."

"What the hell's that mean?"

"In your story on the Kipinski heist, you said his partner's name was Siskowitz."

"Right."

"Wrong. Ziskowitz. With a Z. You got it backwards."

"Big deal! Typographical error."

"Winchell would never make a gaffe like that, Ben." I laughed.

"Fuck you and Winchell," he said, hanging up before I could tell him that everything was not kosher in the firm of Kipinski and Ziskowitz-with-a-Z and that I had a strong hunch that Mr. Z on 47 was up to his curly Hassidic locks in whatever had happened to his partner and the three million dollars' worth of precious crystalline rock from King Solomon's mines, or wherever diamonds came from.

On the way back to my office, I picked up a *Mirror* to see if Winchell had used my Nazi tip, but the sports headline stopped me in my tracks. Unbelievably, Babe Ruth had agreed to take a salary of $25,000 to play baseball for Boston! I thought, God what is New York coming to, to lose Ruth? In Winchell, the item about the Nazis rained orchids on the cops for defending American virtues against guttersnipes who would sell out America for a song, especially one by Horst Wessel. "The leader of the Ratzi thugs, Gerhardt Mueller," Winchell growled, "is spending two days in the slammer. They should conveniently lose the key."

Then on an inside page of the paper I found a tiny item that floored me.

11

Death in a Crosswalk

The item got only a few lines with a headline so small I almost skipped over it: YOUTH KILLED IN HIT AND RUN.

The youth was eighteen-year-old Joshua Sloman of Avenue B near Houston. "Sloman was run down by a car in a pedestrian crosswalk at Houston and Avenue A, only a block from his home, as he was returning from work early this morning," said the item. "He died instantly."

On my way downtown I phoned Ben Turner again to tell him about the item. He said he'd check with his city desk to find out what the *News* had on the accident and promised to meet me at the Sloman house. "They'll be sitting shiva," he said. "In Irish, that's a wake."

"I'll wait for you outside the house, Ben," I told him.

He arrived in the *News* Ford. "Are you thinking that maybe it wasn't an accident?" he asked without preliminaries as he bounded out of the car. "So was I, but I talked to our reporter who checked it out and he says it looked open and shut to him. A hit and run."

Inside the Sloman apartment, where Joshua's family and friends were observing the funeral rituals of their faith, I left the questioning to Ben, most of which was conducted in Yiddish, all of which was in voices so quiet I heard little of it. Later, Ben summed up what he'd found out, which was nothing beyond the obvious—that somebody ran Joshua Sloman down around four in the morning, didn't stop, and the body was found almost half an hour later by a woman walking a dog. "It looks cut and dried, Harry." Ben shrugged.

"A goddamned coincidence which I don't like one damned bit," I replied.

"No one but us knew we'd even talked to the kid!"

"I don't care for what's going on in this case, Ben. First Owney Madden puts in an unexpected appearance and knows a hell of a lot about my business. Now a kid we talked to a day and a half ago is run down in the street. The people I want to talk to are nowhere to be found. It's all very peculiar."

"Who said life is ever anything but peculiar? If you ask me, and I haven't heard you asking me, the accident that killed Joshua Sloman was just that. An accident."

"Mebbe," I said, unconvinced.

"Like I said, no one but you and I knew we'd talked to the kid."

"Not so. The maitre d' at the Rainbow Room knew. And Gloria Seldes knew."

"How'd *she* know?"

"I told her."

"What the hell for?"

"Ben, I work for the lady. She's paying for this case, remember?"

Ben shook his head. "Okay, so you told her because she's paying you to find out who killed her husband. That doesn't exactly add up to her driving around town all night waiting for a chance to hit-and-run Joshua Sloman."

12

House Call

When Gloria Seldes flung open her apartment door, she was wearing a smile. Only a smile. She looked startled to find me there, but not nearly as startled as I was to see her buck-naked in the doorway. "Suppose I were the milkman or something?"

"I don't drink milk." She smirked, stepping back and letting me through the door.

"Do you always answer the door with no clothes on?"

"I was expecting a lady friend. I was dressing because we're going shopping. I didn't expect to find a man a the door, but now that I have found one, I'm not complaining."

"Put something on, Gloria. This is business."

With a chastened shrug, she went into the bedroom and reappeared wrapped in a pink housecoat. "Okay, business," she said and dropped into the corner of her couch.

"I told you about the busboy at the Rainbow Room who had a ruckus of some kind with your husband?"

"Yes."

"The kid is dead. Hit and run."

"Oh, no!" she gasped.

"They say it was an accident," I said, never taking my eyes off her. "I don't believe it."

"If it wasn't an accident, it would have to be ..."

"Murder," I said. I watched for her reaction. She winced at the word. "What do you make of it?" I asked.

"I can't make anything of it. Who would want to murder a kid like him?"

"That's what I'd like to know. Funny, though, that it happened the day after I talked to him, hm?"

"Yes. Scary."

"Only two people knew I was going to talk to the kid. The headwaiter at the Rainbow Room—"

"Why would he want to murder the boy?" she asked.

". . . and you."

"Me?"

"No one else knew."

She giggled. Nervously. The implication of my words finally getting through. Then she turned cold and hard, hurt and offended. "That is a very strange thing you're hinting at."

I cracked a smile. "Look, I know it sounds bad, what I was adding up, but I had to put it to you straight."

"Do you honestly think I had something to do with that boy's death? When did you say it happened?"

"Early this morning. Around four."

"You were with me until two."

"But not until four."

Tears came into her eyes. "Harry, Harry. How could you even think that about me? What reason would I have? I hired you to find my husband's killer. I hired you to . . ." The tears rolled down her cheeks, and her words choked in her throat.

I felt like a heel, and I told her so. "I just had to know for sure, baby. I figured I owed it to us to come up here and put it to you hard, so I could gauge your reaction."

"You're a cruel son of a bitch, Harry."

"Yeah, I know."

"A real scummy bastard."

"Right."

"A prick."

"Yep."

"A . . ."

"Horse's ass," I snapped.

She let a bit of a smile form at the corners of her mouth. "That, too."

"I'm sorry, babe. Really."

The smile widened. "It's okay."

"Forgive me?"

"Forgiven," she said, holding out her arms and letting her pink robe fall open.

I moved to her side. "So much for business."

"Fine," she sighed.

It was past five before we finished.

"Your lady friend you were going shopping with never showed up," I commented.

"Aren't you glad?" she asked and kissed my chin.

"Very considerate of her."

"Maybe she did show up and heard us. You make an awful lot of noise, you know."

"Me?" I laughed. "You were screaming like a banshee."

"You're very good in bed, Harry."

"I try."

"You're better'n most."

"Only better'n most? Not better than all?"

"I haven't tried them all."

"Better than Joey?"

"That's not a very gentlemanly question to ask a widow, to compare you to her late husband."

"I know a story about your husband. It involves a bet."

"Tell me." She chuckled.

I told her about the famous Onyx Club wager relating to her husband's size.

"If Joey'd known that, he would have been very pleased. He was very vain on that particular subject."

"I heard that it was a main reason you married him."

She groaned with shock. "What a dirty mind some people have! Did you believe that tale?"

"Kind of."

"Size was never important to me, Harry. I always went for quality."

"And Joey had quality?"

"He had a few qualities I liked."

"Such as?"

She began to blush. "You're embarrassing me."

"Come on. What qualities?"

"He was very considerate and wanted to make me happy, to do things I like. I know you believe Joey was not much of a human being, but he could be very generous and considerate, especially when he prized someone. He happened to prize me. He was always very proud of being married to me."

"Why did you marry him? You could have had the pick of the crop, seems to me."

"That's what I mean about Joey. He treated me like a person, not just a good lay."

"I see."

"Do you?"

"I believe so."

"He did his best to make me happy, to feel good, and that had nothing to do with the size of his sexual equipment."

"But you had no objections on that score."

"No, but it wasn't the basis of our relationship."

"Sex is important."

"Sex is also more than a man putting his tool inside a woman. It's being tender and affectionate and giving the woman pleasure. It's finding out what pleases a woman and doing those things because the man wants to, not because he thinks it will pay off in pleasure for him."

"And Joey was all that?"

"All that." She snuggled close, asserting herself all along my body. Her voice was her pillow voice again. "How could you have thought that I would have something to do with the death of that boy? I mean, what sense would that make? I want you to find Joey's murderers."

"In my line of work the sensible thing is to assume that the things that don't make any sense make sense." I lifted her hand and kissed her palm. "Does that make any sense?"

"Yes," she said, melting against me like butter over lobster. "It hurts me, though, to know that you don't trust me."

"Oh, don't let that hurt you. I don't trust anybody."

"You can't be as cold as you pretend to be. In fact, I know you're not cold. You've proven that with me."

"The heat of physical passion has nothing to do with the temperature of a guy's heart. If you ever believe it does, you will really wind up hurt."

"I wish I knew you. Understood you, I mean."

"No you don't."

"What are you afraid of? Who hurt you so badly that you have to put up all these defenses?"

"Now you're getting into my history again. Why do women always want to dig into the past?"

"And men don't?"

"Not if they're smart. What a dame did yesterday, before she met me, is as important to me as the tout sheets at Belmont from last season. All I expect is for a dame to be straight with me while she's with me. I don't give a hoot in hell about her past."

"Still, I'd like to know who she was who hurt you so badly."

"Well, I'm not going to go over the past, darling, and that's that."

"You were awfully interested in my past with Joey."

"Because Joey's a case. In a case, the past is important, but only to the case, not to me personally."

"I could be a murderess or a bigamist or an archvillainess of the worst stripe, and you wouldn't care?"

"Are you?"

"See? You do care."

"No. I thought you wanted to play one of your silly little games. I thought this was pillow talk, having nothing really to do with us."

"That's the second time you talked about 'us.' "

"I hadn't noticed."

"A while ago you said, 'I figured I owed it to us to come up here and put it to you hard.' "

"I did say that, didn't I?"

"Us, we are important?"

"In a way."

"There go the defenses up. Like a wall. A sheet of armor."

"It's too soon to know for sure about us."

"You realize that I could care for you a great deal."

"You say you could, but that could be just loneliness talking. Like you said, it's been a long time."

"I could have called up any number of men if all I was was lonely. I called you."

"Yes, you called me."

"Are you glad I called?"

"Yes."

"But?"

"But what?"

"Your tone was that you were saying, 'Yes, I'm glad you called, but . . .' "

"What do you want from me?"

"Honesty."

"That's a two-way street."

"See. You don't trust me after all."

"If that's what you want to think, so be it."

"I don't know what to think, Harry, but I know how I feel, and I have very deep feelings toward you. I'm not playing any games, Harry, and I wish you wouldn't play games with me." She sat up and lit another Marlboro cigarette. From her posture, the way she attacked the cigarette, I knew she was angry. "Perhaps it would be better if I let you call that other detective you said you knew."

I sat up and put a hand on her shoulder. "It's too late for that. I'm on this case to the end, whatever that is."

"Even if I fire you?"

"Even if you fire me."

"I might not give you any more money."

"That won't make any difference. If you think firing me or not giving me any more expense money will protect your feelings, then fire me and cut off the dough. I'll go on with the case. That's for sure. That's for damned sure."

She turned into my arms. She lifted up her head in that cock-eyed way of hers when she was wearing her peekaboo hats, and I noticed how really blue her eyes were, like cornflowers. "You are a very dangerous man, Harry MacNeil."

I kissed her hard. "Am I fired?" I asked.

"You were. But now you're hired again."

13

Inspector of Police

On the other side of Second Avenue in the dusky shadows of the elevated in his unmarked car, slouched down in front in hopes he wouldn't be spotted, Inspector Mike Grady stuck out like a sore thumb. He was beet-red because I'd seen him when I crossed over and tapped a knuckle on the window by his head. "Evening, Grady!"

He rolled the window down a crack and sat up straight. "What do you want, MacNeil?"

"I thought you wanted something, sitting out here in the cold like this, watching for me."

"What the hell could I want from you?"

"Must be something, else why would you be parked here?"

"I just pulled in to get a cup of java in that greasy spoon at the corner."

With a smile, I laid my hand on the hood of his Ford. "The metal's colder'n the proverbial witch's tit. I *am* a detective, Grady."

"That was always debatable, MacNeil."

"Okay, Grady, I'll put it to you straight and simple. Are you tailing me?"

"What the hell for? Geez!"

"I haven't the foggiest idea."

"You ain't worth the time, MacNeil." He sneered, rolling up the window. He pressed down on the starter, gunned the engine, and sped away, lurching into Second Avenue traffic and looking

angrier than I'd seen him in a long, long time—angrier, even than
the day Mayor Walker learned that Grady and I were two different breeds of cops.

James John Walker expected Grady and me to be cut from the
same bolt of policeman's blue. "Your captain is very high on you
fellows." The Mayor beamed from his chair in his corner office
in City Hall. "Your captain thinks you'd do fine as my new
bodyguards." Walker grinned, the puckishness of his Irish soul
emanating from twinkling eyes and across smiling lips. "Now, I
don't believe I need bodyguards. After all, they'll love me in
December as they do in May, east side, west side, all around the
town." He half sang the last words, making a joke on himself
with the lyrics of the songs that were as vital a part of Walker's
Beau James image as his Broadway tailoring, his opening-night
top hat and cane, his gold cuff links, and drop-in calls at any
society shindig that caught his fancy at the Central Park Casino.

"All this noise that the Seabury Commission is making has
some of my boys worrying about me. I don't have to tell you
about the boys and how they worry! They believe it would be
advisable for me to be squired around from now on by a pair of
savvy cops who can be trusted. What do you say? It could be
fun!"

"It's an honor!" exclaimed Mike Grady with his always unal-
loyed enthusiasm for getting ahead.

"What about you, MacNeil?" asked the Mayor jovially.

"I'm not what you call a political flatfoot, Mr. Mayor."

Walker giggled. "That's a hot one. 'Political flatfoot!' There
are plenty of that breed around, eh?"

"Yes, and that's okay, but it's not for me, Mr. Mayor."

"What's the matter, MacNeil? Do you have visions in your
head of someone telling you *sotto voce* to meet some guy over by
the Lackawanna Ferry Building in the dead of night to pick up
a bag full of payoff money?"

"Certainly not, Mr. Mayor!"

"That's good. From what I've been reading in the papers and
hearing in whispers among the press boys in Room Nine, some

characters have the idea this administration's been for sale from day one."

"I wasn't making any kind of insinuations, Mr. Mayor."

"I know. You'd just rather not be a shiny-shoes blue-serge always-have-your-pants-pressed member of His Honor's entourage."

"I guess that's about the size of it." I nodded, thinking that maybe I ought to say out loud that I could never be happy cooling my heels while the Mayor did the town, merely to be on hand to drive him home when he was in his cups and to keep an eye out to be sure there were no reporters around when he stayed the night with his showgirl girlfriend.

"I'd like to have you with me, MacNeil. And I could, just by lifting a finger. You know that."

"Yes, Mr. Mayor, but then I'd have to quit, wouldn't I?"

Walker twinkled. "Yeah, I guess you would."

"I like what I'm doing, is all, Mr. Mayor," I said, trying to take any personal edge off the conversation, which turned out to be unnecessary, because Jimmy Walker understood me very well.

Grady did not understand at all. He blew up in my face before we reached the bottom step in front of City Hall. "What kind of a fucking asshole are you, MacNeil? Insulting Walker like that."

"He wasn't insulted."

"Treating him like a Bowery bum to be shunned!"

"You're taking this personally, which is more than the Mayor did, Grady."

"Well, you made me look like a fuckin' fool."

"How?" I laughed.

"How the hell else could I look? I tell Walker I'd be honored to have the job and you turn around and let Walker think that he's not worth the time of a goddamn lousy flatfoot. That crack about political cops! That sure made *me* out to be one."

"Hell, you are one, Grady."

He stopped in his tracks in the middle of City Hall Park, his angry voice scattered a flock of pigeons. "Just tell me what that's supposed to mean."

"It doesn't mean anything," I said softly, taking another step.

Grady seized my coat, jerking me backward. "You were saying that I'm on the take."

"Bullshit, Grady."

"How else am I to take what you just said?"

"I don't give a damn how you take it," I snapped, tossing off his arm and striding away.

He came after me but didn't touch me again. There was venom in his eyes. "You know, you could have blown my big chance back there. He could have sent both of us packing, the way you insulted him."

"What the hell do you want from me, Grady? You got the fucking job, didn't you?"

"What's important here is that you nearly screwed it up, Mac-Neil. You and your damned holier-than-thou attitude."

I wheeled around, seeing him in all his self-righteousness with the elegant cupola of City Hall behind him, the flags of city, state, and country snapping on the wind, the sky a fair blue, a warmth of spring in the air—all the things that Mayor James J. Jimmy Walker liked to crow about when he went out strutting his stuff and singing his ditties about how great a town New York was, east side, west side, all around.

"I'll say this once to you, Grady. I'm a cop. A flatfoot. I do the job I believe a cop should do, and with me that's keeping my hands in my pockets, not my eye out for a way to line them. I'm not saying I don't take a gift or two at Christmastime or accept an apple or a piece of pie or a cup of java from the people I'm there to protect; but if they give me gifts, it's for thanks, not because I've got my palm open saying 'Gimme 'cause I'm a cop an' I'm entitled.' "

"You sanctimonious son of a bitch."

"If that's what you think I am, fine. I don't give a shit what you think of me, Grady."

"I oughtta do right now what a lot of the men in the precinct and the squad room have wanted to do for a long time."

"What's that, Grady?"

"Punch you in your goddamned mouth."

"You try, Grady, and it'll be the last guy you ever punched."
My hand went to my belt where I holstered my gun.

Grady barked a laugh. "Shit! You'd shoot me? That's a joke."

I tapped the heel of my hand on the butt of the pistol. "As
sure as God created City Hall pigeons, Grady."

Grady made out okay on Walker's staff as long as the job
lasted. I'd see him in the background in Sunday rotogravures or
in the *News* and the *Mirror* and once or twice in the crowd behind Walker in Pathe newsreels. Stalwart and protective in his
pressed suit and shined shoes, a presence around the Mayor
among all the other presences; he was even with the Mayor when,
at last, Gentleman Jimmy had to go up to Albany and sit like a
schoolboy in front of Governor Franklin Roosevelt to answer
embarrassing questions raised by Judge Samuel Seabury's investigation into corruption in the government of the City of New
York. I never followed all the details about the deals and schemes
by greedy men to get richer off the city's transit system or any of
the other plots that came slithering out from under the rocks that
Judge Seabury turned over. Like most New Yorkers, I was at first
amused by the goings on.

I still laughed as much as anyone else much later when the
newspapers printed a particular story about the day the Mayor
got his subpoena duces tecum to bring with him to the Joint
Legislative Committee on May 25, 1932, all records of his personal financial transactions from January 1, 1926, to date. The
newspapers wrote that that morning Jimmy Walker spiffed up
as always in his nattiest attire, climbed into his car for the ride
down to Foley Square, and said to his chauffeur, "Drive carefully. We don't want to get a ticket."

Grady'd gone along for that ride, and for all the other rides,
including the one that led down from Albany to Walker's sudden
announcement that he had sent this message to City Clerk Michael
J. Cruise: "I hereby resign as Mayor of the City of New York,
the same to take effect immediately." The house of cards that
Jimmy built tumbled fast, thanks to the termites who'd been
gnawing away at its foundations for many years.

Michael P. Grady escaped unscathed, going back to police headquarters with the rank of inspector, as political a cop as you could find anywhere in Gotham.

A few months later, I had my name painted on a piece of glass in the door on the fourth floor above the Onyx and put public service behind me.

A few times after that chat in the office of Mayor Walker I thought about Jimmy Walker and how he'd blithely assumed that Mike Grady and I were alike. That had been Jimmy Walker's flaw. He never could read character very well.

The rattle of the Second Avenue el above my head shattered all the thoughts of the past that my most recent run-in with Mike Grady had triggered. My mind snapped quickly and rudely back to the puzzling case of who killed Joey Seldes. The why of it seemed not quite as murky as it had seemed at the start. The why of it now definitely had the allure of sparkling diamonds mixed in. I was certain that if the Kipinski heist was the reason for Joey's demise, it meant that the absent Joe the Dude Dennehy had been behind the rubout. The only fact that didn't fit snugly into my little theory was the words the killers spoke to Joey as they gunned him down—"You were told to stay away from the kid."

That "kid" cluttered up my neat little picture of the rubout at the Onyx Club while the "kid" never came into focus. He had been at Joey's side that night at the Onyx, probably in the gang of toughs picking on Joshua Sloman at the Rainbow Room, and hanging back shyly from getting into conversation with Joey and Sliphorn Kelly at the Cotton Club up in Harlem, yet it was as if the kid existed only in Joey's presence. No one else knew him, as far as I could tell, except—possibly—Sliphorn Kelly.

The Second Avenue el was a distant rolling thunder fading fast downtown as I turned west on Fifty-sixth aiming for the Onyx and home. I was looking forward to a scotch to get the taste of Mike Grady out of my mouth. I was in need of sleep, too, so I'd be fresh when I started out to locate Sliphorn Kelly and to find out once and for all who "the kid" was.

14

Obituary

No torture ever devised by man compares to the hideous torment of a song running through your head and you can't recall the title. The one kicking around in mine and rolling around on my whistle all along Fifty-sixth Street was, I recognized, a Gershwin number from the 1920s, one of his cleverly syncopated show tunes, although which show and which title eluded me. It wasn't until I breezed into the Onyx and whistled the tune for Art Tatum that I realized how music can sneak down into you and stir up the things that are really bothering you. "That's from *Tip Toes*." Tatum nodded, his incredible hands going immediately to the keyboard and producing a Tatum interpretation of the song which, he told me, was called "Looking for a Boy."

When Tatum was finished, I signaled Louie to bring over a beer for the knowledgeable pianist who had ended my torment. Tatum was always a great one for beer. In fact, no one I ever knew then, before, or since could down as much brew as Tatum. Stepping away from the piano, I started whistling the tune again. "You must be damned happy, Harry." Tatum chuckled. "People whistle for two reasons. They're happy or they're scared, and I ain't never know'd you to be scared, Harry."

I was still whistling "Looking for a Boy" when I unlocked my office and went in. I was momentarily disgusted with the wreck Madden's errand boy had made of it, but I was too damned tired and too frustrated by the sight to do anything about cleaning up the mess. I threw myself onto the couch, my head cradled in my hands, and stared up at flickering lights and shadows on the ceiling, hoping that a flash of inspiration would come to me, like one of those lightbulbs over a character's head in the comic strips when an idea is born.

When inspiration ignored me, I reached inside my coat and took out the curious handwritten note that Gloria'd found in Joey's pocket. I still knew very little of what was there in the boyish scrawl. I thought I knew who Mr. Z on 47 was, and that Joey had a safe of some kind which could be opened only with that combination so amateurishly written down. The rest of it was as puzzling as ever. The man's name: Kenny Lambda. Not exactly a name to fit the Italian kid Louie had described as having been with Joey that night, nor the one Winchell had seen at the Rainbow Room. *It is No. 123 in corner* was meaningless. As was *in the corner at the back is the richest jock in town.* I was certain it all had to do with the Kipinski diamonds.

I fantasized about diamonds, what I'd do with three million dollars' worth of them, where I'd put them. "In a safe," I said aloud. How big a safe, I wondered, would be needed for three million in cold blue ice? Not a very large one. Owney Madden was right. Jews in the diamond district were known to walk around with millions in gems in their vest pockets.

It was possible that the diamonds never left the little cubicle where Herschel Ziskowitz plied his trade, I told myself, but in the end I figured that didn't add up, because Mr. Z just hadn't come across to me like a man who had the stones tucked away neatly for sale when the heat was off, when it was safe to put them on the market again.

When it is safe!

Excitedly, I reached into my coat again and drew out Joey's message, looking at the last four words: *when it is safe.* I understood then that Ziskowitz did not have the gems. He was to be visited by Joey, or whoever had the diamonds, only when it was safe. Safe for what? To sell them back to Mr. Z, in all likelihood.

I tucked the note away again, pleased with myself at deciding about that.

No wonder—I chuckled—that Mr. Z was so concerned about an insurance settlement on the missing merchandise. He had to know Joey Seldes was dead and that the diamonds were probably never going to find their way back to him—if that had been the plan all along.

I blinked my eyes a couple of times at the shadowy ceiling and then laughed. "Shit! A crazy scheme! Clever and daring and crazy." I shut my eyes hard a moment, opened them, and stared up. I asked myself out loud, "How could a twerp like Joey Seldes manage a caper like that?"

I got up and went over to my desk, mindlessly straightening it out, while the preposterous image of Joey Seldes as a master criminal amazed me. Gershwin's "Looking for a Boy" whistled off my lips once more, syncopated mockery and irony.

My office was reasonably well reconstructed before I decided to hit the couch again for some sleep. I snapped off the lights and spread out in the dark, aware of faint music from the Onyx four floors down and traffic on Fifty-second Street and the general hum of the city.

Lying on the couch, I silently calculated for my own inspection, contemplation, and evaluation what this case added up to. It started, I told myself, with Joey Seldes always wanting to be a big shot. A hanger-on with the Madden mob. Never a guy with a promising future. Not much better than a gopher. "Hey, Joey, gopher coffee and danish." "Hey, Seldes, gopher a couple a pastramis on rye over at Lindy's." "Hey, Joey, gopher a pack of Spud menthols for Owney."

To the mob, Joey was a chump, like a picture on a wall, someone you would talk in front of if you didn't know about pictures having ears. One day Joey overheard Molloy and Dennehy cooking up a free-lance job. Dangerous if Owney found out. A little piece of info that could be used by a weasel like Joey to cut himself in on the action. The two mobsters hustling Joey by giving him something to do in the scheme. Joey senses that Molloy's a guy with treachery in his heart. Joey warns Joe the Dude that Molloy is planning to cut Dennehy out when the caper is over with. Or vice versa. The two mobsters kidnap Shmuel Kipinski, kill him, grab the diamonds. Their plan is to make a sell-back deal with Mr. Z. Joey might have had that role in the scheme, to set up the deal with Mr. Z. Most of it happens as planned. Then Molloy winds up a corpse out in Coney Island. Dennehy also doublecrosses Joey by sending a couple of hired guns to rub him out that night at the Onyx.

Lighting up a Lucky and staring at its red glow in the dark, I told myself that it was very plausible. It could have happened that way.

Gradually the pieces I'd forced together to make a picture of the puzzle fell apart. If Joey was such a hanger-on in the caper, why did it appear that *he* wound up with the diamonds tucked into a safe whose combination he'd tried to disguise in his pathetic little memorandum? Why did Joe the Dude wait so long to get rid of Joey? How come Mr. Z had never been approached? *Where was Joe the Dude?*

And who was the kid Joey had been palling around with? What was his connection?

Had he been in on the Kipinski kidnapping and murder? And there was more.

Where the hell was Joey's safe?

Who the hell was Kenny Lambda?

Where were the Kipinski diamonds?

Where was Kipinski?

Where was Joe the Dude?

How come Owney Madden was back in town?

Where in New York City was Sliphorn Kelly when I had to talk to him so bad?

I got up and went down to the Onyx to let the music drown out all the questions that I had no answers for. It was late. Early, really, in the morning, and the joint would soon have to close so someone could turn on bright lights and sweep out the place and carry out the empty bottles. The final tunes were mellow, the jazz free. A handful of musicians from the 3 Deuces had come over to listen. Johnny Mercer, a young guy with a clever talent for lyrics and melodies, was tilted against a wall on a chair that looked like it was about to collapse. Jack Robbins, the publisher everyone called Mr. Music, was in. Lou Levy, the talent manager, was nursing a nightcap. It was a very relaxed crowd, and I knew that it wouldn't be long before one of them would say, "Let's go uptown for some yardbird and strings," lingo for chicken and spaghetti, and then a visit to Dickie Wells's spot on East 136th Street, a favorite after-hours jamming local for Onyx habitués.

Behind the bar, Louie, who always seemed to be there, was toweling the mahogany and looking forward to locking up. "A hard day, Lou?" I asked, leaning in my usual spot, a scotch in my hand.

"No harder'n usual. You look especially beat, Harry."

"It goes with the territory, Louie."

"Me and a couple of guys are goin' across the street to our favorite cathouse. Join us."

"Nah. Not in the mood."

Louie frowned. "Let me guess. A bad case of the Black Widow blues?"

"No sermons, Louie, please. It's late."

"Hey, you get no sermons from me. Now don't get me wrong, Harry, but I figure this Seldes dame only hired you because she was a long time without regular banging."

I groaned. "What a lousy mind you have, Louie."

"It's my only asset."

"Well, you're off base about Gloria. She's not as bad as you think."

"Mebbe so, Harry."

"You think I'm being a sap? Go ahead, say it. You could always level with me, Louie."

"I got nothin' more to say. We all have to lie in the beds we make for ourselves."

"Isn't that the truth, Louie?"

"I read it once in Winchell," he said, barking a laugh and then yelling out across the club, "Closin' time."

"Who wants some yardbird and strings?" came a voice from the back.

Once upon a time, it would have been an irresistible temptation, but I was dog tired now and had too many questions kicking around in my head to be fun to anybody up in Harlem, so I climbed up four flights and hit the hay.

Around six, Ben Turner woke me out of a sound sleep by phoning from his desk in the city room at the *News*. I felt sorry for Ben when he worked nights at his newspaper while other folks jammed. "You awake?" he asked.

"I am now."

"Good, 'cause I'm meetin' you in front of your place in my car in ten minutes."

"What's up, Ben?" I was awake now, for sure.

"They found Joe the Dude."

I was on my feet and reaching for my coat. "Where?"

"A floater in the East River over by the Con Ed pier at Fortieth Street."

"I'll meet you there."

"I told you, Harry. I got the car. I'll pick you up out front of the Onyx in ten minutes."

"Ben, did they find—"

"No diamonds, Harry."

How they knew it was Joe the Dude was from a label in his jacket with his name embroidered on it. Without that, a quick identification would have been impossible. Weeks in the water made for chancy recognition. How they knew he'd been there for weeks was a rolled up and pulpy *Daily News* in his pocket. Only bits of it were readable, but one bit was the date. *December 27, 1934.*

"That kicks my theory right in the ass," I muttered to Ben as we hung back with a knot of reporters and photographers while the cops tried to make the handling of a six-week-old water-logged and bloated corpse as easy as possible on themselves.

Ben suggested, "He could have ordered Seldes bumped off and ran into this bit of bad luck *after* he hired the gunmen."

"Nah. He had to have been killed the same night that Molloy bought it out in Coney."

Ben nodded and allowed as to how that made sense. "Do you suppose Joey did this?"

That would have seemed laughable at one time. "Mebbe." I nodded.

Ben strolled away for a couple of minutes to be a reporter, joining others of his breed to form a little knot of questions around a sergeant from a midtown precinct whom I didn't recognize. In a while, Ben sauntered back, flipping the pages in his little reporter's notebook and sliding a stubby Eberhard Faber under his hat above his right ear. "It looks like Joe the Dude was shot, but only the coroner can decide that for sure. Looks like a bullet hole in his vest, though."

"Are they going to try to match the bullet in Joe and the one they got from Molloy?"

Ben lowered his voice conspiratorially. "I didn't want to ask that question with those other reporters around, Harry, but later this morning I'll call a guy I know in the morgue and put it to him. He'll give it to me exclusive that way, see?"

"Ask him if the bullets could have come from a Colt Government Model .45."

Half an hour later, I was sitting with my chin against my fists and staring at nothing in particular while Ben made music of his coffee at the Sandwich Man as a dull yellow morning faded in beyond the windows where people hurried past in increasing numbers on their way to jobs, those lucky enough to have them. For Ben, this should have been the end of the day, but I knew that finding Joe the Dude in the East River meant he'd have to drive out to Queens for a third and final interview with a gal named Mary Margaret Mulligan, for whom this would turn into a day she would never be able to forget. Nobody needed to read in the papers how Mary Margaret Mulligan felt when she learned that her fiancé had been fish food for six weeks, but it would be included in the story that Ben would write for the next day's paper, because Mary Margaret Mulligan had been part of Joe the Dude's life, no matter how slightly, no matter how superficially, no matter how ignorantly. I had no idea if Ben was thinking about Mary

Margaret Mulligan or not as he slurped the paint-remover java, but I'd known Ben a long time and I would have put down a lot of dough that he was if you'd've asked me to bet on what he was thinking about. What he said finally was "What's your next move?"

"There's only one. To find Sliphorn Kelly and hope he can put me onto this mysterious kid that Joey'd be palling around with."

"Does it still add up to the Kipinski diamonds?"

"I don't know. Maybe you were right all along. That Joe the Dude and Eddie Molloy were just mob business, nothing more. I wouldn't be surprised if Herschel Ziskowitz-with-a-Z has his partner's body stuffed under his workbench and the gems tucked in his vest pocket."

"I can vouch for there being no body in Mr. Z's place of business, 'cause the cops gave that a really professional going-over. Your pal Grady was in charge."

"I didn't know he'd been on the Kipinski case."

"Only that first day, I think. The investigation was taken over by another inspector for some reason or other."

"That son of a bitch has been tailing me."

"What the hell for?"

"Who knows? All I know is, he was around the other night—last night—after I'd paid a call on Gloria."

Ben leered and wiggled his eyebrows like Groucho Marx. "Say, is it turning into something between you and her?"

I didn't answer, because I didn't know.

"Well, I'm not surprised. She's a gorgeous dame," Ben said.

"She's been lonely, as you might imagine."

"A woman like that ought never be lonely. If she's ever lonely and you're tied up, give me a call, pal."

"Hey! Gloria Seldes isn't kosher."

"Hell, neither am I. Haven't been since I moved off Avenue A."

"I'll keep you in mind if I ever need a stand-in."

"No you won't, Harry. You're serious about her."

"What are you? Some kind of swami? See all, tell all?"

"I know about these things. I recognize the signs."

"What signs?"

"With you, it's setting aside your customary aloofness, your icy-cold detachment about a case. You've got a passion for this case, Harry. It's rare to see. It almost makes me believe that someday someone could get through to you on a really intimate level."

"Shit! Listen to Dr. Freud! I thought you were a crime reporter, not a goddamned Miss Lonelyhearts!"

Ben's eyes twinkled. "I wrote one of those columns once. I had to fill in while the regular guy was on vacation. I'll take a floater out of the East River every day rather than write that drek."

I slapped down a half a buck to cover our breakfasts and walked out of the greasy spoon with Ben to stand with him on the corner looking through the brightening dawn at the tall, gleaming, impressive *News* building. Suddenly I was feeling damned good about being in New York and being friends with the best crime reporter in the business and being who I was and what I was, even if I had been knocked back to square one in the maddening mystery of who killed a pipsqueak nobody named Joey Seldes, who was turning out to be the most surprising and interesting character I'd ever come to know. "Call me when you hear from your buddy in the coroner's office," I said, slapping Ben on the back.

"I'll do that, Harry."

I ran for a trolley and rode across Forty-second to a Broadway that was deader than Joe the Dude at that hour on a frosty-bright February morn.

15

The Sliphorn Blues

Before I had a chance to phone her about the finding of Joe the Dude, Gloria Seldes read about it in the afternoon papers and called me up to tell me about it, jingling the phone almost off my desk and jolting me out of blissful unawareness around three in the afternoon. She was breathlessly bewildered. "What's it mean, Harry?"

"I don't know what it means. Where are you?"

"Saks."

I had a vision of her trying on peekaboo hats and driving the salesgirls crazy. "What time is it?"

"Ten to three."

"Have you had lunch?"

"I never have lunch. I'm watching my figure."

"Great. I'll have lunch and watch your figure with you. I'll meet you by the statue at Rockefeller Center. You know the one. The naked guy. If I'm late, you can stare at him and think about me."

"Don't be late, Harry!"

As it was, I wound up waiting for her. It was nearly four when she strolled down the Promenade, around the skating rink, and over to me leaning on the wall above the head of the statue of Prometheus. She was emptyhanded. "I thought you'd been shopping?"

"I had everything sent."

"That's real class. I do my shopping down at Union Square and usually wear the stuff out the door."

"I'll bet you do!"

"It's true, 'cause by the time I get around to buying new duds, the ones I have are falling apart."

"You and Joey are different on that score. He was very interested in clothes, and I used to—" She cut herself off because she could see that I wasn't interested in her talking about Joey in the hay and making comparisons. She smiled fleetingly, and then tossed off any embarrassment with a shake of her rusty-red hair. "Where are we dining?"

"You pick it."

"Schraffts."

"*Schrafft's?*"

"I'm going to be very bad and have ice cream."

We walked over to Broadway, where I thought we'd most likely find a Schrafft's. She pleased me by twisting her arm around mine. I looked at her sidewise, seeing her in profile. "You're a damned good-looking woman, Gloria."

She cocked her head. "I know."

A little put off by her attitude, I said, "But you have a lousy coloring job on your hair. You ought to get it done by someone else."

She squeezed my arm. "How would you like me as a blonde?"

"I think I'd like that. Yeah. I would."

"I'll transform myself into Jean Harlow. Platinum blonde."

At Schrafft's she ordered coffee. "What about the ice cream? How about a hot fudge sundae?" I asked.

"Platinum blondes mustn't be fat." She winked.

Again, as she had at the Commodore, she avoided mentioning the case. Instead, she babbled about Harlow and about the movie star's handsome leading men, and about John Mack Brown and Wallace Ford and James Cagney and, with adoring eyes and awe-filled voice, about Clark Gable. "He's got such sexy ears!"

"Ears?" I laughed. "Since when are ears sexy?"

"Oh, Harry, surely you know the joke about the Frenchwoman and the ears?"

"No." I chuckled.

She slipped into her pillow voice and leaned toward me over the

table. "It goes, 'How does a French woman hold her liquor?'
Not L-I-Q-U-O-R but L-I-C-K ..."

"I got it already." I winced.

She closed her eyes. "Oh, to hold Clark Gable by the ears!"
With eyes closed, she tongued her lips. Her eyes popped open
and she smiled. "I've shocked and embarrassed you."

"No. Just got me to thinking."

The eyes narrowed, the voice growled. "As Red Riding Hood
said, 'What big ears you have!'"

We hailed a cab in front of Lindy's.

Around ten, I said, "I gotta get outa here. There's work to be
done. Work you happen to be paying for, darling."

"That was a terrible thing that happened to that Dennehy
man." She shuddered and pulled the sheet up to her neck. "Be
careful, Harry."

"I will, darling. You can count on it."

We kissed and I left her there wrapped in the sheet while I
grabbed a taxi to go back to my office and change shirts and try
to decide the best place to start looking for Sliphorn Kelly. Naturally, I glanced in at the Onyx bar and there sat Ben Turner.
"Mind if I tag along while you turn the town upside down in
search of Sliphorn?" he asked. Then he added, "Nothing from
my pal at the morgue yet on the bullets. Maybe tomorrow."

Ben waited a little longer at the bar while I changed, then we
started scouring midtown for Sliphorn, checking out the clubs and
rooms where a nigger could play in the band but couldn't come
in as a paying customer. We began at the Roosevelt Grill, where
Bernie Cummins's band was playing, but Bernie hadn't seen Slip
in nearly as long as I.

At the Piccadilly on Forty-fifth, Wingy Mannone said he remembered seeing Sliphorn a couple of weeks ago. "He was jivin'
after hours in one of the joints on The Street, but I haven't seen
him since. You know about Sliphorn and the dope, how he gets
his hands on some of that poison and just vanishes until it's all
used up and he's sober. You might check with Jack Denny over
at the Biltmore. Jack was looking for a pickup trombone player

a few days ago. Maybe he found Slip. No better trombone man than Sliphorn."

But Jack hadn't seen Sliphorn either, he told us after Ben and I spent some time waiting while Ray Heatherton sang and the novelty and dance acts came on, featuring Vivian Vance, Barry DeVine, and Florence and Alvarez. Ben turned antsy during the dance routines, and soon we were headed outside without a clue as to where to find Sliphorn. Ben was pretty much in his cups, a condition that as often as not led him into recitations of "The Face on the Barroom Floor."

"Where to now?" he asked, a little pie-eyed as we paused by the curb on Madison by the Biltmore.

"Now," I said, jamming my hands into my pockets, "we take the A train."

It figured that Owney Madden would have taken an interest in a place like the Harlem Cotton Club, Owney being a character with an instinct for the natural connection between good booze and good music. During Prohibition, Owney had heard about a place uptown at 142nd Street and Lenox Avenue where there'd been attempts to turn an upstairs dance hall into a club. One attempt had been by the boxer Jack Johnson, who opened a spot called the Club Deluxe, not with a great deal of success.

It was Owney's interest in developing a Harlem outlet for "Madden's No. 1" beer that turned the club around and set it on the road toward success as the Cotton Club. The Cotton was converted into a spot where whites from downtown were entertained by Negroes in dazzling shows featuring flashy dancers, gorgeous girl singers, and jazzy bands. Duke Ellington's band made its first big hit there, followed in 1930 by Cab Calloway and his "hi-de-ho" style. Great singers such as Ethel Waters sang there. And Lena Horne. Shows were written by white writers and composers who went on to bigger successes on Broadway—Harold Arlen and Dorothy Fields and Jimmy McHugh. In those days it was whites in the audience and the Negroes up on the stage, but the color bar loosened somewhat in 1932, so the relatives of folks in the show and famous Negro entertainers could come in through the front door as well as the stage door.

The band featured at the Cotton as Ben Turner and I traveled uptown in the A train was Jimmie Lunceford's, a classy orchestra. His name was up in lights on a square marquee with a huge lazy "C" in the word "Cotton" looking like a fishing hook. The pavement beneath the marquee was awash in bright light. A noisy cluster of downtowners filed through the doors, up the stairs, and into the horseshoe-shaped club where the seating capacity had been stretched to the limit by jamming tiny tables together, and therefore putting the customers elbow to elbow on two tiers overlooking the dance floor and the incredibly tiny stage. The decor was plush, with a strong hint of the primitive—just the kind of atmosphere after-hours whites from downtown expected when they went uptown slumming.

Ben had a drink or two while I scoured the place for anyone who might have seen Sliphorn Kelly lately, all to no avail, both among the waiters out front and the entertainers backstage. They all knew the fabulous Sliphorn Kelly, but none had seen him in a while. I figured someone in the Lunceford band might know, but I had to wait for the band to take five during an intermission, so I joined Ben at the table and had a scotch. While waiting, I kept an eye on Ben for signs of any eruptions of "The Face," but he was blissfully wrapped in the music.

When the band broke for five, Lunceford came over to the table. Elegant in a white suit à la Cab Calloway, a pinky ring glinting gold and rubies, his teeth as bright as pearls in a smile that would have conquered the world if his music hadn't, he exclaimed, "Hey, Harry!" He laughed, brushing a finger over his tiny mustache. "You're doin' some uptown slummin' tonight, I see!" We were pals from 1934, when he'd premiered his miraculous jazz orchestra at the Cotton, featuring the greatest sax player I'd ever heard, Willie Smith.

"I'm looking for Sliphorn Kelly."

"Ooo, that little viper." Jimmie frowned. He eyed Ben Turner and felt moved to explain. "A viper is a cat who smokes reefers."

"I know," snorted Ben, nodding and a little sleepy-eyed from too much booze.

"Ben knows the score. He writes for the *News*. Ben, this is Jimmie Lunceford, jazz immortal."

"Immortal!" Lunceford laughed. "Say, that's somethin'!"

"Have you seen Slip around?"

"Nope. He could be on a toot."

"I'm afraid that's what it looks like."

"It sounds important, Harry."

"It is."

Lunceford thought about it, then said, "You'll want to look for a cat named Candyman. Hangs out at a fried chicken place, 125th and Lenox. He peddles what Sliphorn buys."

"How will I recognize him?"

"He'll be the sober one. Gotta go, Harry. Dig ya later."

By the time we walked into the chicken joint at 125th and Lenox, Ben was sobering up and feeling famished, so we partook of the southern fried chicken while I kept my eyes peeled for a likely candidate to be the Candyman. He ambled in around one o'clock, carried out a couple of transactions near the door, and kept looking toward me and Ben in the back. He smelled a cop; but when I walked over to him, he stood his ground, a slender black man, about thirty, I figured, in a dark blue overcoat and a battleship gray fedora.

"Are you here to roust me?" he asked with the sublime patience and forbearance of the frequently arrested.

"I'm looking for Sliphorn Kelly, who's a friend of mine."

"What makes you think I'd know where he's at?"

"Jimmie Lunceford said you'd probably know."

"What do you have to do with Lunceford?"

"We're pals. Look, do you know where Sliphorn is or not?"

"Don't get huffy, man. I have to be careful. I have a responsibility to my customers to keep outa jail."

"It's important that I locate Sliphorn."

"Well, if it's that important . . ."

I slipped him five bucks. "Your info better be right."

"You gotta go downtown these nights to find Slip."

"I've been to all the downtown joints."

Candyman snickered. "Not those joints, man."

"Where is he, already?"

"Down on Queer Street. In the Village. You know what I'm talkin' about?"

"Tell me."

"There's a bar on Macdougal Street. It ain't got no name on it or nothin'. It's a no-name bar. For queers. Did you know Sliphorn was queer?"

I didn't, but I snapped, "Does that make him a bad person?"

"No, just *queer*, man." Candyman giggled. "You don't look queer. You look like a cop."

Angry, I said, "Jackass! What's it to you what I am?"

On the A train downtown, Ben had a good laugh. "You sure do run into some characters, Harry!"

16

Queer Street

What two people did in bed was no skin off my nose, I figured. Besides, finding out Sliphorn Kelly was queer was not exactly a surprise. Plenty of musicians were queer. I knew that. Everybody knew that. If being queer had anything bad to do with music, I didn't know what it was. It seemed to me if being queer did have something to do with making music, it was something very positive. It seemed to me that you have to put your soul into making music plus your suffering and your pain. The queers I'd known had enough of each to make an awful lot of good music.

Ben and I got off the subway at Fourth Street and Sixth Avenue and walked a block to Macdougal. This was Ben's turf. He lived on the other side of Washington Square, a few blocks away. He told me he thought he knew where this no-name dive was. "I've been past it a couple of times but thought it was out of business. It always looked closed. Besides, when I'm this near to home and need a drink, I have it at home." We turned on Macdougal toward Bleecker and passed the Provincetown Playhouse, sadly dark because of the bad times. It had been a great place to go for plays. You'd have expected the Provincetown Playhouse to be in Provincetown, and it was until 1916. That year it moved to 133 Macdougal, into what had been storehouses, a stable, and a bottling works. Going past, I hoped times would turn better soon so that places like the Provincetown could open up again.

A few feet along, Ben Turner pointed at a nondescript wooden door and grunted, "I think this is the place."

I studied the plain brown-painted door. "Well, there's no name on it."

Ben grabbed the latch, pulled, and the brown door swung open. Inside, we found a long narrow room with a mahogany bar down one side and small tables with red and white checkered tablecloths down the other. Dim bare bulbs punctuated the middle of the ceiling. At the back, a dirty red sign identified the portal to the men's room. A pall of cigarette smoke choked the place. Along the almost deserted bar, bar stools stood in rigid abandonment. Only two were occupied, at the far end, by two slender young men. Shadowy figures under the dim lights and through the smoke; they looked up at Ben and me as we came in, studied us a moment, then turned back to each other and resumed their muffled conversation.

A blond young man behind the bar walked to the end nearest us. "May I help you?"

"Do they call this place the no-name bar?"

"Some people do," the young man replied. "It's late. We're about to close."

"I'm looking for a guy."

The young man's face crinkled with amusement. "So?"

"A lanky fellow, very likable, name of Sliphorn Kelly."

"Am I correct in assuming you are a police officer?" the young man asked.

I was about to tell the young man that what I was was none of his business, but I spied Sliphorn stepping out of the men's room. "Never mind, pal. There he is now," I said, striding the length of the room with Ben Turner keeping up.

"Hey! Slip! It's Harry MacNeil! Been looking all over town for you!" I could see he was loaded.

He grinned and swayed a little and nodded hello to Ben when I introduced him. We sat at one of the checkered tables.

Sliphorn Kelly handed me his reefer. "Take a drag on this, Harry, an' you an' me'll sit aroun' and chew the rag like the old days, eh?"

I much preferred booze to marihuana, but I took the little brown cigarette and inhaled the sweet, harsh smoke, holding in the smoke awhile to let it work. Ben politely declined. Sliphorn had taught me reefer smoking years before, when I was still with the police and hanging around speakeasies on Forty-ninth Street before they all were pulled down to make room for Rockefeller Center. Sliphorn had played trombone in one of the dives and had shifted his talents up to Fifty-second along with everyone else. Sliphorn was really a Negro, although he looked white and passed for white in bands before it became respectable to have Negro bands in downtown joints. The last name—Kelly—fooled a lot of people. Sliphorn's old man had been an Irishman who skipped out on Sliphorn's mother when he found out the luscious charcoal beauty was pregnant and when she refused to have an abortion.

I let Sliphorn's marihuana work on me for a minute or two before I got down to the business that brought me around to see him. "Pops Whiteman told me you could tell me something about Joey Seldes."

"Whatcha wanna know?" Sliphorn grinned.

"You can tell me to go to hell in case this gets personal."

"There's nothin' too personal between friends, Harry."

"Pops told me that a few weeks ago he saw you and Joey Seldes up at the Cotton."

"Yeah. I was there. Joey was there. I was playin' well, Harry. You oughta heard me."

"Pops says you and Joey had a talk."

"Yeah, we did."

"And that there was a young kid with Joey?"

Sliphorn took a deep drag on his reefer, choking a little from the sting of the smoke but holding it in, then exhaling with obvious relief and great pleasure. "A young kid?"

"A Dago-looking kid, probably."

"Ah, that number! Yeah, he was a very good-lookin' kid. I fancied that kid a lot."

"Do you know his name?"

"Let me think about that a minute. It don't come right to my mind. I remember seein' him though. Really a good-lookin' boy.

I envied Joey a lot bein' with that boy. I don't think the kid cared much for me, though. I guess I wasn't his type. Bein' a nigger. I once knew a boy like him, down in the South. Southern boy. He liked me a lot. Of course, I was much younger then, but that boy and I had quite a few good times together. He didn't mind I was a nigger as long as he got what he wanted, if you know what I mean."

"About the kid Joey was with?"

"Just can't think of his name, Harry. Maybe Joey never told me his name. Oh, he was a very handsome boy, and I sure wouldn't've minded knowin' that boy. No sirree."

"What were you and Joey talking about that night?"

"Ah, nothin' important."

"It could be important to me, Slip."

"Well, Joey wanted to impress his boyfriend, you know?"

"Impress him how?"

"By fixin' it so the kid could try some dope."

"Joey wanted to buy dope for the kid?"

"Yeah. They said they were goin' to a party of some kind. What you might call an orgy. The kid wanted some good dope to take along, and Joey'd told the kid that he knew where to get some."

"Did you get the dope for them?"

Sliphorn grinned. "I surely did, and they were very grateful."

"Did you happen to find out where that party was? That orgy?"

Sliphorn giggled, smoked, exhaled, and giggled again. "Only party those two was goin' to that night was between theyselves."

"There was no party?"

"Oh, I'm sure they was a party. For two."

"The two of them were going to get doped up together?"

"For starters."

At that point, Ben Turner exploded with impatience. "Harry! Don't you get it? Joey and this kid were queer for each other!"

Sliphorn giggled ."They surely was!"

Incredulous, I shook my head. "Joey Seldes? A queer?"

Sliphorn clucked his tongue. "What they call a switchhitter."

Ben spoke up again. "Are you certain that's what was going on between Joey and the kid who was with him at the Cotton Club?"

"It takes one to know one," Sliphorn replied preachily.

Ben and I looked blankly at each other a moment. "That's a hot one," I said finally. "I'd've never guessed that about Joey. Not in a million years. With a wife like that?"

Sliphorn slapped the table and laughed wildly. "Shit, Harry, where you been all your life? Who says a guy can't be queer *and* married?"

"Nobody says it, I guess, Sliphorn."

"You are such a chile sometimes, Harry."

"Hey, Slip, when are you going to sober up and go back to work, back to your horn?"

"Soon, Harry, soon, but I got a little more forgettin' to do."

"Forgetting?" asked Ben.

"Yeah. Every now and then I forget I ain't white and then somebody reminds me, so I take some time off to blot out everything about myself except that I'm a nigger queer who likes his dope. Dig it?"

"Dig it," I replied.

"Dig it," Ben echoed.

"Vito," muttered Sliphorn.

"Beg pardon?" I said.

"Kid's name is Vito."

"Vito," said Ben. He looked at me. "Sounds right for a Dago."

"Did Joey mention his last name?"

"Mebbe. I can't rightly say."

"How about Dacapua?" I asked. Ben gave me a startled look. I told him what Winchell had told me about a kid by that name who wanted badly to be connected to the Luciano mob but his big brother objected. "Could his name have been Vito Dacapua, Slip?"

Sliphorn was down to the tiniest stub of a reefer and holding it gingerly between thumb and forefinger, sucking in mouthfuls of air in hopes of catching the last wisp of marihuana smoke. "I only know his name was Vito," he said, exhaling. He stared for a moment at his tattered little piece of brown paper, empty of the weed. He sighed deeply. "That's the last of it. I'm outa weed and outa scratch." He looked at me with baleful eyes. "Could you lend me a buck so's I can get a bed in a flop house round the corner, Harry?"

I reached over and squeezed Sliphorn Kelly's bony shoulder. "I have a couch at my place. You can sleep on it tonight, Slip. In the morning, you'll eat and go over to the Y for a shower and then you'll go back to playing your sliphorn. Okay?"

He shook his head and began to sob. "I can't do that, Harry. I hocked the horn. That's what paid for the weed and the dope." Huge tears rolled down his gaunt cheeks. "It was good dope, Harry, but I used it all and that was my last reefer and my horn's in hock! That is God's gospel truth about me, Harry."

"We'll get your horn tomorrow, Slip. C'mon."

With Sliphorn walking unsteadily between us, Ben and I went over to Sixth Avenue, where I hailed a taxi. "Where are you going to sleep if you give him your couch, Harry?" Ben asked, helping me load Sliphorn into the cab.

"I got a floor," I said. "Get in. We can drop you."

"I can walk it. Save the fare. Give it to him."

I climbed in the cab but held the door open a moment to say to Ben, "This is one of the great trombonists of all time, Ben. The least I can do for a man who plays a horn like that is let him have the use of my couch, hunh?"

17

"Looking for a Boy"

I decided to let Sliphorn sleep it off, but before I left my office the next afternoon I went through his pockets and found the dog-eared receipt from the pawnshop on Eighth Avenue where he'd hocked his trombone. I slipped the ticket stub into my wallet and drew out one of the twenties Gloria Seldes had advanced me. I laid it beside the couch on the floor where Slip could find it, along with a note telling him to eat and get cleaned up and then wait for me until I got back. I had a lot more questions to ask him about Joey, the "kid," someone named Kenny Lambda, and all the other loose ends to this little ball of twine Gloria Seldes had dumped into my lap.

It was late afternoon when I went out looking for the "kid." Vito, Sliphorn had said, was his name. Now I had to find out if Vito could be the brother of the Luciano torpedo named Dacapua whom Winchell had told me about. Winchell, I figured, was the place to start. From what I knew of his habits, he'd be at home brushing up his column before sending it by messenger to the *Mirror* in time for its six o'clock press run. I arrived at his Central Park West apartment house expecting a hard time from the door-man, but when he buzzed up to Winchell and mentioned my name on the lobby phone, I heard Winchell's raspy voice. "Send him up!"

He came to the door to let me in. He was in a white shirt and tuxedo pants, but the shirt was open at the neck and braces hung

97

down in loops at his sides. He was in his stocking feet. "Hi ya, Harry. I'm just getting dressed for a shindig at the Astor. La Guardia's speaking tonight. I can't miss a La Guardia speech 'cause you never know what the Little Flower is going to say. Come in. I wanted to thank you for that tip on the Ratzis down by the library. Good item. It turns out the sleazy bastards have really got themselves an organization. They take their orders from their guttersnipe Führer over in Berlin, of course. I'm gonna lambaste them every chance I get in the column. Maybe I can get Roosevelt and his cronies and the rest of the country to wake up to what's going on over in Hun land. But you're not political, are you, Harry? Care for a drink?"

"Scotch."

Winchell poured. "What brings you around, Harry?"

It was fine scotch. Smooth. "The other day at Hanson's you told me about a Luciano hood name of Dacapua."

"Right."

"And you mentioned a younger brother. Happen to know his name?"

Winchell puzzled it over, but I wasn't sure if he was just trying to remember if he knew the kid's name or trying to dope out what my angle was. "I don't recall it, I'm afraid. Important?"

"Could be."

Winchell's mouth slowly curled into a sly smile. "Ah, was he the kid you said was with Joey Seldes the night Seldes was killed?"

"You keep coming back to Joey Seldes, Walter."

"Harry! Everyone on The Street knows you're digging into that nothing event, so what am I to think? I'm no dummy, you know. You say Seldes was with a young kid. Now you ask me about the younger Dacapua. It adds up. And to four, not five." He leaned back in his easy chair and shook his glass, making the ice tinkle. "Harry, I'm not going to use any of this in the column, so don't worry about opening up with me. I know your cop's heart is wary of newspapermen."

"Walter! Some of my best friends are newspapermen."

"How *is* Ben Turner?"

"He sends you his regards."

Winchell exploded in a laugh. "That little cocker! Hates my guts! That's why I love him so."

"You're sure you don't know this Dacapua kid's name?"

"I can in a minute if you want me to find out." He reached for a white telephone on the table at his elbow. He lifted the receiver. "One call will do it." He saw my uncertainty and added, "I'm just calling someone down at the *Mirror* who'll look in the files."

"Okay." I nodded, still not entirely certain if I was doing the right thing. It was a couple of minutes before Winchell got an answer over the phone. In the meantime, I got up and poured myself another scotch. Winchell was laying the receiver in its cradle when I came back to my chair. "The kid brother's name is Enzo."

"Shit," I muttered.

Winchell grinned and clapped a hand on his knee. "Enzo... Paolo...Vincenzo...*Vito*...Dacapua. Those who truly love him call him Vitelloni. He's eighteen, looks fifteen. Lives by himself in royal style at Patchin Place down in the Village. His brother bankrolls him. Now you owe me one."

Leaving, I had no doubt at all that Walter Little Boy Peep Winchell would collect the I.O.U.

Patchin Place is one of those living-space jewels tucked away in hidden little corners in Manhattan. This one opened off West Tenth Street between Sixth Avenue and Greenwich Avenue, near the minaret-style Jefferson Market Courthouse. A neat row of brick houses faced a couple of ailanthus trees in a courtyard kept private by a wrought-iron gate. It was, indeed, royal digs for an eighteen-year-old kid.

Vitelloni Dacapua was not at home when I dropped by, so I waited across the street by the Women's House of Detention, freezing my tail off until midnight. The kid arrived home behind the wheel of a British Morris PA-type racing car. He was not alone in the two-seater. The young man with him seemed acutely embarrassed when I dashed across the street, caught Vito Dacapua by his sleeve, flashed my wallet with its investigator's ID, and said in my threatening cop-on-an-official-investigation voice, "Vito, I have a few questions to ask you about the murder of one Joseph the Dude Dennehy."

Even before Vito could protest that he knew nothing about the demise of Joe the Dude, I could see in his face that he didn't know what the hell I was talking about. But the gambit was enough to frighten away Vito's pal, who made a hurried excuse and said he'd call Vitelloni tomorrow. Young Vito Dacapua took only a moment before he unleashed a profane and venomous tongue on me, winding up by proclaiming with certainty that "You ain't even a cop!"

"Vito, I know about you and Joey Seldes."

Without batting an eye, he snapped, "You don't know nothin', and who the fuck you think you are comin' around to my house?"

Quietly I said, "Vito, I don't want to talk about this out here in the open, but if you want to have all your nice polite neighbors know you're a queer, I can raise my voice, too."

"Who the hell are you?"

"Name's MacNeil, private investigator."

"I don't know anything about anyone named Joe the Dude, and Joey Seldes was just a friend."

"Not the way I heard it. Shall we talk in your house?"

"Make it quick. You just ruined my evening."

"He said he'd call you tomorrow."

"Up yours, private dick!"

I decided being polite was getting me nowhere, so I grabbed Vito by his Brooks Brothers lapels. "I got enough evidence right now to connect you with the murders of Eddie Molloy and Joe the Dude, a diamond dealer named Kipinski, probably a kid named Sloman, and the theft of three million dollars in diamonds that a nasty little gangster named Owney Madden would like to collect for his very own. Now, shall we talk or shall I just call up the cops, or maybe Owney the Killer, and give 'em your address?"

Vito reached up and respectfully loosened my hands from his overcoat lapels. "Come inside."

The parlor was what Ben Turner would call piss elegant: white sofa and chairs, glass-and chrome tables, modern lamps, a couple of the chic modern-style paintings consisting of various lines and squares and blotches of color that you saw all the time in Madison Avenue galleries and which looked like something a kid could do as well. Maybe it was being in his familiar surroundings that changed him, but suddenly hard-as-nails Vito Dacapua turned into a pussycat, taking off his coat and offering to take mine, pouring a couple of glasses of white wine, and opening a black lacquered cigarette box to invite me to try one of his Players English cigarettes. I declined in favor of a Lucky. He sat in the corner of his white couch. I stood in the middle of the room looking down at him. I thought he looked like Valentino must have looked when he was eighteen, very dark and brooding and with a beauty that was almost but not quite feminine. I could easily understand what Joey Seldes had seen in the kid, given what I now knew to be Joey's flexible attitudes toward who he screwed. "Is it true you and Joey were, uh, lovers?"

"Yes."

"Tell me about it."

"What more is there to tell?"

"I want to know all about you and Joey Seldes from the day you met to the night he was rubbed out with you standing beside him at the Onyx club."

Vito cracked a grin. "You know I was there."

"I found out you were."

"You must be a very good detective, Mr. MacNeil."

"About you and Joey?"

"We met at a party in an apartment in Brooklyn Heights late last summer. I'd been spending the summer with a few friends in the Hamptons, and it was the weekend when they had to come back to the city. They'd closed up their cottage for the season early. The party was to be their plunge back into the city life, given by a man who is a Broadway producer.

"His friend—lover, if you will—is an actor. The actor and I grew up together. He's how I first came to understand what I am. Queer, if that's the word you will best understand! I was at the party for about an hour when my producer friend and my

actor friend got to talking about another guest who was coming
to the party but who was late. They said he was famous for being
extremely well hung. He was coming with a young man who had
met him, also last summer, and who had begun introducing this
man around to various persons in our little clique.

"I never cared much for the guy who was bringing the well-
hung fellow. He was named Gary, or something like that, and
was one of those blond Adonis types who were never much to my
taste. Do you know the sort? Golden hair, blue eyes, all muscle
and teeth, like a Pepsodent ad? I was surprised that an all-American number such as Gary would arrive with someone who wasn't
good-looking at all. I mean, Joey Seldes was beyond common.
He looked somewhat like an animal, if you know what I mean.
Since it wasn't Joey's outward appearance that made him so pop-
ular, I assumed it was Joey's other physical endowment that
attracted Gary to him. As well as to all others.

"Naturally, I was interested, so I made it my business to get
to know Joey—shall we say intimately? All the rumors were true!
Then I found out he was connected to the Madden mob! He was
never very much in the gang, as far as I could tell, but he talked
a lot about how he was going to be a big shot one day. I never
paid much attention to it.

"Until just after last Christmas. He came to see me around
that time to bring me a gift. I expected something ordinary. A
shirt or a bottle of after-shave. Only Joey comes into this very
room, reaches into his pocket, and comes up with a *diamond*.
Not a tie clip or a ring with a chip or anything as penny-ante as
that! This was an unset diamond as big as the tip of your little
finger. I couldn't believe my eyes! I asked him where he got it,
and he boasted that I should check out the newspapers and I
could read all about it. Maybe you saw the papers at that time?
About the disappearance of the diamond merchant. The papers
said he had been carrying around three million dollars' worth of
diamonds!

"Well, I began to have a little more respect for Joey Seldes. He
told me he had the diamonds and had stashed them where no
one would find them. He said when things cooled off he was going

to be a very important man in this town. Very important. He kept saying that. Then he said when he was a big shot he'd take me to Europe and out to Hollywood. It sounded fine to me. I was ready to go along with him. Then we went out New Year's Eve to celebrate, and those guys came into the Onyx and gunned him down. I got my ass out of there in a hurry."

"Do you know who killed him?" I asked.

"Now you're getting into things I'm not going to gab about."

"I take it from that that you do know who did it."

"Like I said, I'm not telling you any more."

"Your brother did it, didn't he?"

"You better go now, MacNeil."

"Your brother's very protective of you. He fixed it so you couldn't get into the Luciano mob, which is what you really wanted, right? He set you up in this house. He bankrolls you. Mother-hens you all down the line. I guess that he knows you're queer and that's damned embarrassing, so he does what he can to be sure you don't get hurt or make a fool of him or ruin the family name. Does that sound right, Vito?"

"I got nothing to say."

"The way I see it, your brother really screwed up, though."

"Oh, yeah? What're you getting at?"

"Well, he seems to have bumped off Joey before anyone found out where the diamonds are stashed. That's what you were planning on finding out, I figure. You were really impressed by Joey having a part in that diamond deal, but then that devious mind of yours starts working. You decided to go along with Joey's scheme to travel to Europe and on out west, but all along it was your plan to get your hands on the diamonds and then dispose of Joey yourself. Your brother screwed that up."

"That's an interesting theory." The kid smiled.

"You made a mistake by not telling your brother all about Joey and the diamonds. Maybe you tried, but your brother just didn't want to hear anything about you and your association with Seldes. After all, Seldes was a two-bit creep. Worse, he was a Madden mobster. And a queer on top of it. Maybe if you had let your brother know that Joey had pulled off the biggest caper in

this town in years, your brother wouldn't've been so quick to erase
Joey Seldes from your life. That is, not until you'd found out
where Joey'd stashed the ice."

"What's your angle, MacNeil?"

"I don't have any angle. I'm just working for Seldes's wife,
who wants to find out who killed her husband and why."

Vito laughed. "Shit! Do you mean to tell me you fell for that
dame's line about how she loved Joey? Is that what she told you?
You're not the detective I just gave you credit for being. She
hated Joey with a passion. Oh, not at first. At first she was very
lovey-dovey with him, although I don't know why. Maybe she
likes big men!

"The honeymoon didn't last long. They fought all the time.
Especially after she found out about Joey and me. She made a
really nasty scene up at the Central Park Casino when she discovered Joey and me having dinner one night late last year. She
just happened to walk in that night with a guy, spotted Joey, and
came over to really rip into him. She even slapped him. Right
there in public. Well, Joey would never stand for that, so he cold-
cocked her. Right there in front of the world. Flattened her. Then
the guy she was with stepped in, and he would have creamed
Joey if Joey hadn't pulled the automatic he always carried. So
much for widow's tears, MacNeil."

He broke into a smug smile, then started to laugh. Just as
suddenly as his laughter started, he turned serious again. "You've
got no proof for any of this, you know. There's no way you can
hang Seldes's rubout on my brother. No way."

"You could testify to it, Vito. You knew your brother was behind it. That's why you got your ass out of there so fast. Oh, I'm
sure your brother didn't do it personally. He probably got a
couple of gunsels from the Luciano mob, a couple of buddies.
That's who you recognized, am I right? You knew the two birds
who blew Joey away and you knew that your brother was behind
it. Only thing that puzzles me is, Did you ever tell your brother
what a sap he was? Did you ever tell him that he'd killed the guy
who was going to lead you to three million in diamonds?"

Vito laughed again. "Wouldn't that have been a joke on big
brother? A hot one, for sure."

"You know, Vito, I haven't seen so much brotherly love since Cain and Abel."

"It's a very funny situation, isn't it, MacNeil? Here we are, a couple of smart characters talking about Joey Seldes, who both of us used to think of as not very bright. Yet Joey turns out to be smarter than you and me put together. He may be dead, but he went out knowing he'd pulled off a really big deal. It's funny. Don't you think?"

18

Widow's Tears

Very funny. Only I wasn't laughing. I never saw a lot of humor in being played for a sucker, which is how I pictured myself as I waited on the subway platform for a train to take me uptown again. The thought that kept running through my head was that Gloria Seldes had told me at least one lie—about not having any idea about Joey palling around with a good-looking Italian. If she'd told one lie, chances were good that she'd lied to me in other ways.

It was late when I arrived at her place and found the door locked and no answer when I leaned on the doorbell, so I made up my mind to wait. I parked myself on the stairs that faced her apartment door. The outside door to the building was half a flight down behind me, so I couldn't see her when she came into the lobby, but she wouldn't see me waiting, either, which is what I wanted. This little visit I wanted to be as big a surprise as my visit when she'd flung open the door stark naked. I was hoping to catch her naked again, in a way.

I must have sat for an hour before I heard a car pull up outside. There were two voices, muffled, but I recognized hers even if I couldn't hear the words. Next minute, she was inside and up the half flight of stairs and fumbling in her purse for her key. "You've been out awfully late," I said.

She jerked with fright and spun around, her face ashen. She dropped her keys. "Harry!" Her fright turned to surprise and relief. "You gave me a start."

106

I stood up on the bottom step and towered over her. "How come you lied to me about never having seen Joey with a good-looking Dago kid?"

She flashed a nervous smile. "But I didn't lie to you." Her hand went up to her rusty hair, patting it. "What makes you think I lied?" Then she bent down and scooped up her keys. When she straightened up, she was as composed and calm as ever. "If I said that to you, and I guess I did, perhaps I was mistaken. I may have forgotten." She waited for me to say something, but I kept my mouth shut to let her worry about the big silence between us and about what I had said and what I might be thinking.

"Joey knew so many people. Mobsters. Cheap guys. I never paid much attention. They were always trying to put their hands on me. One of them might have been the person you described. I never meant to be absolute if I told you, uh, when I told you I'd never seen Joey with the boy you described." She smiled again, but without the nervousness. I recognized the smile. Her come-on smile. Like the one when she told her little joke about men's ears. "Well, aren't you going to come in and tell me all about this mysterious *Dago,* as you refer to him, and when I saw him and what he has to do with my late husband?"

"Yeah," I said, coming off the step, "maybe we should go inside."

She handed me the keys and I opened the apartment door. It was softly lighted from a lamp in a corner. "I always leave a light on. I don't like coming home in the dark," she said, breezing into her parlor and going around turning on more lights until she was at the bedroom door. She paused and wiggled her fingers at me. "Just a sec'." She came back a minute later without her coat and hat, straightening a belt around her waist and smoothing out her red dress. The big ring on her finger sparkled in the light. A strand of real pearls made a graceful curve above the valley between her breasts. "Drink?"

"That'd be nice," I said. I took off my coat and dropped it on a chair by the door, then went over to her couch and sat, watching her from behind as she poured a scotch for me and a gin for herself. "You've been out on the town?"

"A quiet dinner with an old friend."

"Boyfriend?"

She turned and smiled nervously again. "Yes. You don't know him."

"Maybe I do."

"Is it important?"

"No."

"Good." She smiled, handed me my scotch, and sat beside me, her legs folded under her, her gin in her hand resting on her knee. "Now, what's this all about? Why are you so angry with me?"

"I don't like being lied to, baby."

"I didn't lie. Really. I merely forgot."

"Well, I can see how someone could forget meeting someone casually."

"Certainly."

"Only I don't see how anybody could forget getting cold-cocked in the middle of the Central Park Casino and getting knocked down on her pretty fanny." I looked at her sidewise. She was a study in composure. She sipped her gin, then reached out and set it on the cocktail table in front of the couch. She sat back calmly. "Not to mention Joey pulling a gun on the fellow you were with that night."

"You *are* a good detective, Harry."

"One of the best, darling. I'm even better when I get the straight dope and my clients don't lie to me."

"Yes," she sighed. "I didn't tell you the truth about that boy."

"Tell me the truth now."

"I never knew the boy's name. He was an Italian, as you said, but that's all I knew. That and how handsome he was. That face should be in the movies. Anyway, I saw the boy only once. Suddenly, I believed rumors I'd heard. You see, I knew about Joey's women, and I could deal with that. Neither he nor I were virgins when we got married and neither of us expected to give up a lifetime of sleeping around. We had that understanding going into our marriage. We didn't put restrictions on each other, because we knew that if we did the marriage wouldn't stand a chance of surviving. When we were together, it was magic. When we went

our separate ways and then came back to each other, it always
seemed better between us.

"Occasionally I heard that my husband liked boys as well as
girls. At first I dismissed the gossip as just that. Gossip. It wasn't
until I'd gone out for dinner with a dear friend, that evening at
the Central Park Casino, that I saw Joey with a young man. He
was a boy, really. I think that was what shocked me more than
anything else. The boy was so young. I was confused and hurt
and ashamed, so I made a fool of myself by confronting Joey in
public. He hit me. The man I was with had no idea what was
going on and, being a gentleman, he attempted to help me. That's
when Joey pulled a gun.

"Later, Joey was filled with remorse. He actually cried as he
begged my forgiveness. He told me he would never do it again.
He said he only got into that situation because the boy was well
connected and could help Joey get ahead. Only there was a price
to be paid for the boy's help. Joey said it was no different than
a dame in show business going to bed with a producer or an agent
or a director in order to get a role. He said that by being nice to
that boy he could move up in, well, Joey's kind of work.

"The reason I didn't tell you about it was because I was frankly
ashamed. It was over with, so it did not seem very important to
me. Obviously I was wrong. I had no idea that that boy was that
important to you in the investigation. Had I known, I would have
told you everything, but I didn't see any value in giving you the
impression that my husband was a flaming fairy. He wasn't. He
told me that everything I'd heard about a string of other boys was
lies put out by his rivals in the gang. He said the only time he
ever got mixed up with a queer was with that Italian boy. He
swore it was the truth, and I believed him. As far as I know,
he never saw that boy again."

"Joey was with the kid the night he was killed."

"You must be wrong about that."

"No. Joey was with the kid that night."

"Whoever told you that was lying to you."

"The kid told me himself."

"Oh, God! I don't think I want to hear this."

"Baby, you hired me to find out who shot your husband and why. You paid, darling, and now I'm going to deliver the goods."

"Let it go, Harry. Please."

"I can't do that. This has gone too far. There's too much at stake in this, now. People have been murdered. Joey and those two mobsters he was working with and maybe that Sloman boy. Not to forget old Shmuel Kipinski. There are grieving widows and a brokenhearted gal in Queens to square things for. And there are three million dollars in diamonds somewhere in this burg waiting to be claimed. And I might even say that some thought ought to be given to serving justice.

"No, I can't drop it, darling. Not even if it breaks your little heart. It's very endearing to see how you want to protect what little reputation Joey had by not owning up to the fact that he went in for queers from time to time. Okay, I can understand that, but I deal with the truth, darling, and truth comes unvarnished. Maybe I should have spelled that out to you in stronger terms at the very beginning; but you understand it now, so I'm putting you on notice that if you've lied to me about anything else in this case, what Joey did to you up at Central Park Casino is child's play. Got that?"

"Very clearly."

"Excellent. Now, you are going to get the unvarnished truth about Joey. You paid and you're entitled, whether you're willing or not to listen. First of all, Joey wasn't playing around with that kid because he thought the kid could help him get ahead. It was just the opposite."

"Oh, Harry, that's ridiculous!"

"You just listen, darling. Okay? The kid, whose name is Vito Dacapua—by the way, a brother of a gunsel in the Luciano mob —went for your husband in a big way, if you'll pardon the pun. That was just for openers, however. Later the kid learns that stupid little Joey Seldes, everybody's gopher, has got his hands on three million in gems. He gave the kid one for Christmas. Did Joey give you a rock for Christmas, Baby?"

She shook her head. "Whitman's chocolates. I threw them out."

"Jesus, I just hope he hadn't stuck a diamond inside each one as a clever little surprise!"

"Oh, God! Do you—"

"A joke, baby. No. The diamonds are in that safe for which we have the combination. I'm certain of that. We find the safe, and we find Joey's diamond mine."

"Harry! *Three million!*"

"Minus the rock Joey gave his tight-assed little Wop lover."

"Have you found the safe?"

"Not yet."

She snuggled close, snaking her arm in mine like the day we went to Schrafft's. "Three million. Thinks of the possibilities if you find the safe. The possibilities for us."

"Oh, I'll find it."

Excitedly, she giggled. "Do you have a clue?"

"I'm working on it. I found that little Dago queer, didn't I?"

"Three million dollars, Harry!"

"Oh, you'd never get full value. Maybe half that if you found a fence. A pretty good reward from the insurance company if you turned in the stones."

She squeezed my arm. "Why turn them in?"

"Oh, you are devious."

"Who would ever know if you found them?"

"Yeah, that's right. Why, you might not even know."

She blinked her eyes a couple of times. Then I smiled. She pinched my arm. "You tease!"

"First, we'd have to find the stones before we decided to do the honorable thing, or the dishonorable thing, whichever way it came out to be."

"You're the detective!"

"Yeah."

"You must have some idea where Joey would have a safe?"

"Not a bit. All I have is one last name to check out. The name in Joey's note. Kenny Lambda. I hesitate to ask if you know anyone by that name."

"I don't, Harry. As God is my witness."

"I warned you what might happen if you lie to me again."

"Why would I lie now?"

"Well, you might be thinking about finding Kenny Lambda yourself and making a deal with him for the gems."

"You are a lousy-minded—"

"We've already made a list of what I am."

"I'd never doublecross you, Harry."

"*No* you *wouldn't!*"

"How am I going to make you believe that I care for you a great deal?"

"I'm not sure, but I'd bet that we'll get the answer to that question when I find Joey's stash."

"Kenny Lambda." She mulled the name for a moment, then brightened with an idea. "Maybe he's in the phone book!"

"I looked. He isn't."

"Well, I'm sure you'll find him," she announced confidently.

"I hope so. He's the last lead I have."

"The last? Suppose you can't find him?"

"End of the line, baby."

19

Reprise: The Sliphorn Blues

She begged me to stay the night and I let myself be persuaded, but I was awake early and on my way down to lower Eighth Avenue to Rothman's pawnshop to reclaim a trombone. Gloria was extremely warm and contrite and it was difficult to leave, but I told her there'd be plenty of time for forgiving pillow talk once I'd located Joey's stash. "I can't find Kenny Lambda while I'm screwing you, honey," I whispered as I rolled away from her.

"And he *is* your last clue." She sighed.

"Yep," I said.

It was a lie, of course, because Vito Dacapua had mentioned the name of another of Joey's boyfriends, a blond Adonis named Gary; but I saw neither the virtue, the need, nor the wisdom in relating that additional scrap of info to my client, especially when I was no longer certain whether I could trust Gloria or precisely what her game was. I was pretty well convinced that Gloria's objective all along had never been revenge and justice for her slain hubby but the whereabouts of the diamonds written up in the *News* article Joey had so carefully tucked into a pocket. At first, I only suspected that was her motive. I had left open the possibility that her true reason for hiring me was to get to the bottom of Joey's demise, the diamonds being secondary. Now, walking toward the Second Avenue el, I was certain that Gloria had her heart set on enough jewelry to deck out all the kings and queens in Europe. I'd seen avarice in other people's eyes plenty

113

of times, but I never saw it sparkle with the diamondlike hardness I saw in hers as she murmured to me over and over again, "*Three million,* Harry!" I suddenly understood how Adam must have felt when Eve handed him the apple. The concept of temptation had never been put across by my elementary school nuns in quite the way Gloria Seldes put it over.

The pawnable items of a society gone broke clogged the windows of Rothman's at 149 Eighth Avenue as I walked in beneath the big sign that suggested that if you were broke all you had to do was "Call on Uncle." Trouble was, the country wasn't calling on Uncle. The country was yelling Uncle. The man at the counter seemed surprised and delighted that I'd come in to reclaim an item. "It's a fine instrument," crooned the scrawny clerk as he gently opened the lid of Sliphorn's battered black carrying case to show me that the horn was inside. The mellow brass glinted with all the warmth and color that Slip put into the music he made with that crazy concoction of tubes. I paid the guy five bucks, and was depressed to realize how little Sliphorn had sold his soul for. Five bucks had bought the very essence of Sliphorn Kelly. Three million had been the price on Shmuel Kipinski's life. And Eddie Molloy's. And Joe the Dude's. And Joey Seldes's. Not to mention the fact that Gloria Seldes was available for trade, her for the gems, but Sliphorn Kelly had handed over his trombone for five dollars' worth of dope. Going out to the street, I remembered something a cop named Lew Valentine had told me once. "We're all whores in the marketplace, Harry. We've all got a price." I shook my head in disagreement and told the guy, who was now the Commissioner of Police but was then a flatfoot like me, "You haven't sold out, Lew." He chuckled and slapped me on the back and said, "That's 'cause no one's come up with the right price yet!"

The sky had suddenly become slate gray, the clouds hanging low and biting off the top of the Empire State Building as I took the train uptown. By the time I was hurrying along Fifty-second Street with Joey's trombone case swinging in my hand it was snowing. It was too early for the Onyx to be open, and all the other clubs along both sides of The Street seemed cold and lonely and forsaken. The snow slashed into my face. It seemed as if the temperature dropped a degree for every step I took. A dusting of white covered my hat, my shoulders, and the black trombone case by the time I pushed open the door to the stairway up to my office. The heat in the stairs was stifling all the way up.

At the top of the stairs, I stopped dead in my tracks.

The door to my office was open a crack, letting a slant of light spill out into the hallway. I slid my hand under my coat and touched the cold reassurance of my snub-nosed .38, which I slid deftly from holster to hand, my finger curled loosely around the trigger. I took a step closer to the door and paused to listen.

There wasn't a sound from inside.

Then I remembered that Sliphorn had been sleeping off his binge. I'd left a note telling him to wait for me. That had been yesterday. Nearly twenty-four hours. Relieved and feeling a little stupid, I decided that it was Sliphorn in the office, so I tucked my pistol back under my armpit, pushed open the door, and went in.

The place was a wreck.

I thought, That's impossible, because I put everything back after the visit from Madden's errand boy. Yet there it was. Like a hurricane had gone through. The desk was the only thing upright. My file cabinet was tipped over, the drawers hanging out like dogs' tongues in August, my files scattered like autumn leaves. My two chairs lay on their sides amid the paper. The phone from the desk dangled toward the floor. The desk lamp which had been casting its slant of light into the hallway was knocked over, the green shade as cockeyed as one of Gloria Seldes's hats. The couch was overturned.

Sliphorn Kelly was under it.

He was a mess. An unconscious pile of blood and bruise and swollen eyes and split lips and shallow breathing. I thought, At least he's alive!

I uprighted the couch, pulled the pillows from atop the splayed body of the greatest trombone player I'd ever heard, and knelt beside him. "Slip?" I said, reaching to him and touching him where I thought it would hurt the least if he suddenly woke up.

I knew enough not to move him. Anyone beaten up as badly as he was had to have something broken, and I'd learned from being the cop on the scene at countless car accidents and other carnages not to disturb anyone who might have broken bones.

I righted the phone, pressed down on the little bar in the cradle, and listened to the receiver for a dial tone. It came and I dialed for the operator. When she came on, I told her I needed an ambulance in a hurry and gave her the address.

They took Sliphorn over to Roosevelt, and I rode along in the back of the ambulance. The guy in white who rode in the back said he'd rarely seen anything like what had happened to Slip, except a bad elevated accident a couple of years ago. "It wasn't fists that did this," he told me. "My guess is he took a hell of a pistol whipping. Maybe a blackjack, too, for good measure. He must've made somebody awfully mad for them to do that to him."

I said, "Slip never hurt anybody, except maybe himself. He's a musician. A man with a beautiful gentle soul. Plays a trombone."

The guy in white shook his head. "With those split lips, he won't be playing a horn for a long time. If ever."

For most of an hour I waited in a room with brown walls, wooden benches, and the smell of antiseptic and medicine. I left the waiting room outside the emergency room for no more than two minutes to locate a place where I could buy a pack of Luckies.

A few minutes after I came back, a doctor barged out of the room where they were treating Sliphorn. "What the hell happened to that guy?" he asked without preliminaries.

"I don't know, doc. I found him that way."

The doctor looked at me as if he'd heard that tune before. He was a man about my age. He'd been around, I could tell. He took a breath and seemed to require enormous effort to do it. "I don't know about a prognosis. He's badly beaten. Serious internal injuries. We'll have to rebuild his face if we can. He ought to be dead. He by rights should be unconscious, but he woke up a minute ago, asked where he was, asked where his horn was, and asked to talk to a guy named Harry. 'Sthat you?"

"Yes."

"I'll give you thirty seconds with him."

Slip looked like a mummy in all those bandages. He talked in a whisper, hardly moving his lips, like a ventriloquist. "Some mess, pal. Don't know who did it. A big cat. Lookin' for you."

"I gotta be quick, Slip. I have a name to ask you about. Kenny Lambda."

With painful effort he said, "You got it wrong. Not Kenny Lambda. Kenny *at* the Lambda."

"*At* the Lambda? What's the Lambda?"

"Turkish bath."

"Where?"

"Downtown."

The doctor appeared at my elbow. "That's it."

"Where, Slip? Where downtown?"

"That's all, mister!" insisted the doctor, hand on my elbow.

It didn't matter, because Slip passed out. Panicked, I looked to the doctor. "Hey, is he—"

"We gave him morphine. He's just sleeping."

"You take care of him, doc, no matter what it costs, okay?"

"It's my job to take care of people no matter what it costs, mister."

"When will I be able to see him again?"

"I couldn't say right now. As far as I know, you'll be lucky if the next time you see him it isn't at his funeral."

In the lobby, I found a phone booth and a directory, but there was no listing of any place called Lambda. I dropped a nickel in the phone and called the operator. "I need a number and an address for a place called Lambda. Maybe *The* Lambda. In Manhattan." I waited a moment. The operator came on again and said she had no listing of any such place. I told her there had to be a listing. It was a business phone, probably. "It's a Turkish bath," I explained. No, she said. No phone listed for anything resembling a place of that name. Then she said, "Perhaps they have a coin-operated telephone. A pay phone." I asked if she had listings for pay phones. She put me through to her supervisor, who asked me to wait while she checked. Finally, she said, "I have a listing for a pay phone for a Lambda Society at Seven West Twenty-eighth Street. Could that be it?"

"I don't know, darling, but I'm sure as hell gonna find out," I told her.

I hung up, retrieved my nickel when it came back, and stepped out the front doors of Roosevelt Hospital. At the bottom of the steps, in a swirl of snow, his arms folded across his barrel chest, stood Inspector Michael P. Grady. "You don't do nothin' but collect trouble, do you, MacNeil?" he said as I came down to him.

"What the hell're you doing here, Grady?"

"How's Sliphorn?" he asked.

"He's in really tough shape. He may not pull through."

"Why is it, MacNeil, that the people you know wind up ambulance cases?"

"You didn't answer my question, Grady."

"I'm a policeman, MacNeil. When somethin' bad happens in my neck of the woods, I have an obligation to check into it."

"Sliphorn's none of your business."

"Anybody who gets beat to a pulp in midtown is my business. The badge I got in my pocket makes it my business. When someone gets beat to a pulp in *your* office, that makes it my business. The fact that I can't stand your guts also makes it my business. Clear?"

"Then why the hell aren't you conducting an investigation to find out who beat up Sliphorn?"

"Oh, I thought I *was* conducting such an investigation."

"Do you think I pulverized Sliphorn?" I laughed.

"I wouldn't put anything past you, MacNeil."

"Go screw yourself, Grady." I took a step away. He grabbed me. I turned on him. "Hands off, Grady. Understand?" I stepped right up to him, barking steamy words at him through the snow. "I don't know what the hell your game is, why you're on my tail, but I don't like it a bit."

"I repeat my question, MacNeil. How come the people you know wind up chopped meat on a stretcher? Hunh?"

"If you have something to charge me with, charge me."

"Oh, won't that be a happy day? I go to sleep at night and dream about that day. It'll happen, MacNeil."

"Fuck off," I told him as I stepped past him and put up my

arm to flag down a passing taxicab. I looked through the rear window and watched him walk over to the curb, get into his car, and pull away. He stayed behind me as far as Fifty-second, but when my cab turned east, Grady continued downtown. I'd given the driver the Onyx address in case Grady decided to follow me. Now that he was heading in another direction, I told the driver to turn for Twenty-eighth Street.

The Lambda Society was a huge gray building looking like a warmed-over Greek temple on the south side of Twenty-eighth just off Broadway toward Sixth, but as the taxi slid to a stop in front, I could see that the place was closed. There was a sign stuck to the inside of the glass in the door. "Wait a minute, cabbie," I said and got out to have a look at the sign.

It said, HOLIDAY HOURS. OPEN AT SIX P.M.

Climbing back into the cab, I asked the driver what the hell holiday it was.

"Lincoln's birthday," he replied, adding, "Where to now, buddy?"

"The Onyx Club," I told him.

Heading uptown, I thought, Lincoln's birthday. What a joke! I thought about Sliphorn Kelly, an all-right nigger caught in all kinds of traps, and I said to myself, Lincoln freed the slaves, but he didn't do them any favors.

With each block that whizzed past the taxi window, I got more and more steamed. Things had gotten out of hand, I said to myself, watching Herald Square go by, a blur of car lights and dashing people and swirling snow. There was no earthly reason for anybody to hurt Sliphorn Kelly except for the accident of his being in my office when some guy had come looking for me. He could have let him go unharmed. I wasn't there. He could have come back. Instead, he decided to pound on Slip as he gave my place a going-over, which he could have done without laying a hand on Slip.

The question was, Whose torpedo did it? The stunt was something Owney Madden's henchmen were capable of, but Owney's errand boy had already given my place a thorough searching to no avail. Owney was smart. He obviously believed that I had the

Kipinski diamonds, but his futile search of my office would have convinced Owney that the gems weren't there. It added up that someone else saw a reason to pay that call on my office for, I assumed, a look-see to find out if I was stupid enough to have a fortune in stolen rocks there for the taking.

The taxi stopped at Forty-second for a red light. Pulling out, the tires struggled for traction in the deepening snow while the driver cursed nature and all its wonders for making earning a buck so much harder.

If Owney Madden hadn't caused the wrecking of my office and Sliphorn Kelly, I was thinking as we moved more slowly up Sixth Avenue, then who had done it?

As the cab eased into Fifty-second Street, I had no answer to that question.

20

Messages

The Onyx was open for business as usual. As they liked to say at the post office, "Neither rain nor snow nor gloom of night." Drinkers thirsted no matter the weather. The bar of the Onyx was well peopled. Louie was earning his tips. He gave me a nod that told me he had messages, so I parked myself at my customary leaning place and waited. He was thoughtful enough to bring a scotch when he came down to my end of the bar. "Ben Turner called to say he'd be here at six and would wait fifteen minutes. Otherwise he'd leave a message. You gonna be here at six?"

"Here or upstairs. One or the other, I'll be around."

"He said to tell you he got an answer from his friend downtown."

That would be about the slugs dug out of Molloy and Dennehy. I was sure they'd be the same caliber. There was not a shred of doubt, now, that Joey Seldes had used his Colt automatic to deprive Two Fingers and the Dude of their booty. Much to the amazement of Molloy and Dennehy, I'm sure, I thought. "Any other messages?" I asked Louie.

"She didn't call, Harry." He smirked.

"Up yours, Louie."

"Nothing else in the way of calls."

"Did you by chance see anyone going up the stairs yesterday, last night, this morning? Up to my place, that is?"

"I didn't, Harry. Terrible thing, about Sliphorn."

"I assume the whole street knows?"

"Word gets around, even about something that happens when the joints are closed."

"Was Grady nosing around?"

"I didn't see him. Could be, though. I sleep late."

"That bastard's been tailing me."

"How is Sliphorn?"

"Not good."

"Geez, what a crime. The thug who did it was after you, hunh?"

"Seems likely."

"What the hell have you gotten into, Harry? I hope you're not traveling light."

"I'm equipped," I replied, squeezing my arm against the gun under my shoulder. Louie seemed relieved as he moved away to take care of a customer.

It was too early for music and too dangerous to get drunk, so I decided to kill the time waiting for Ben by going upstairs and rebuilding my office.

At a quarter after five, she called. "How's it going?"

"It's snowing out."

"I wasn't asking for a weather report. I wish you hadn't told me. I've been asleep all day and haven't looked out. Now I don't want to."

"Could be a regular blizzard from the look of it."

"What about the case?"

"Nothing since this morning when I left you." I decided not to mention Sliphorn, because it wasn't her concern.

"You didn't find Kenny Lambda?"

"Not yet." I also decided not to tell her that it was Kenny *at* the Lambda who I was looking for.

"You sound awfully gloomy. Are you still mad at me?"

"Nah. It's the weather."

"Are you going to be busy on the case even on a snowy night?"

"I have a few things to do."

"And then?"

"I'll give you a call."

"Maybe I won't be home." She was playing one of her games. "This ain't high-heel weather, darling. You'll be home. Just keep a pot of coffee warm and toss an extra log on the fire. Papa will be there when he can."

"Oh, that sounds so damned romantic! You know what, honey? When this case is over with, we ought to rent a cabin away out in the woods somewhere, get away from everything, and—"

"That'd be something to see! You in the woods!"

"The trouble with you, Harry, is you don't have any imagination."

"Maybe not, but I have a nice set of ears!"

Around five-thirty, somebody was coming up the stairs. I didn't take any chances. I stood with my back against the wall next to the door, my hand wrapped around my .38, and the muzzle at belly level in the direction of the window in the door. There was no mistaking the silhouetted profile that appeared through the opaque glass.

Ben came in without knocking, paused, and whistled through his teeth. "What the hell went on here? Harry? You in there?"

I stepped into view as I was tucking my gun away. "You're early, Ben."

He shut the door and slouched with his hands on his hips, pushing back his open overcoat and his open jacket, a stance that greatly emphasized his middle-aged paunch. With a look of profound disgust on his face, he cracked, "I can't say I'd recommend your way of redecorating."

I uprighted a chair for him. "Second time in a couple of days I've been paid a visit. First was one of Madden's gunsels."

"This time?"

I sat behind my desk and propped my feet on it. "I haven't puzzled that out yet." I reached down and pulled open the bottom drawer where I kept my scotch, which had come through both searches of my premises unscathed. As did a pair of water tumblers stolen long ago from a room at the Algonquin when I'd been on a surveillance of a showbiz celebrity. "The bullets? From Joey's gun?"

"Both forty-fives." Ben nodded. He sipped the scotch and made

a face. "You ought to get a Frigidaire if you're going to enter-
tain. I like my scotch on ice."

"Stick it out the window."

"I've stuck it in a lot of places, but never out a window.
Cheers!" He swigged the scotch as though ice had never been
invented. "I'd like to hang around, but Captain Patterson thinks
I ought to show up for work again."

It occurred to me that I hadn't told him about Slip. He listened with barely contained fury, then banged a fist on the arm
of his chair. "I like that character! Damn, that gets my dander
up. Who did it? Any idea?"

"Not a clue, but if the past couple of days is any sample, half
this fuckin' town knows my business."

"You ought to have an office in some building somewhere,
Harry. With a secretary and regular hours. Four flights up from
a gin joint isn't conducive to the orderly conduct of business."

"I've been thinking about it."

"Sure you have!" He set his emptied glass on my desk and
stood up, buttoning his overcoat snugly over his paunch. "What's
on your agenda tonight?"

I told him about Kenny at the Lambda.

"It smells like another one of those queer establishments."

"Possibly."

"Give me a call later if you want to."

"I will, my friend."

Close to six, I headed downstairs on my way back to Twenty-
eighth Street. On the way down, I ran into two of Owney Madden's boys on their way up. "Mr. Madden would like to see you,"
said the shorter of the two, a pug named Casey. Whether that was
his first or last name I had no idea. He'd been with Madden
about ten years. The other guy was unknown to me. Younger,
surlier, impetuous, and, therefore, dangerous, he didn't say anything in words. He simply drew a gun from his overcoat pocket.
Casey saw the move and sagged a bit with irritation. He pushed
down the hand with the gun. "Put it away, Fred. Harry and Mr.
Madden are friends. Correct, Harry?"

"From way back, Casey."

"We got a car out front," Casey said, stepping aside, back against the wall, to let me pass.

We all rode in the front, Fred behind the wheel, me in the middle, Casey on my right. Fred was mum. Casey had a few tart observations about the deal that was going to take Babe Ruth to the Boston Braves.

Owney was waiting in elegant tranquility in the Terrace Court of the Waldorf-Astoria. He wasted no time as I sat down at his table. "I am prepared to pay you ten cents on the dollar for the gems. That's three hundred thousand dollars, and you don't have to worry about how to get rid of them."

"I worry a little and I have three million."

"You could finance a nice funeral with three million, Harry."

"Before we go on with this discussion, Mr. Madden, I have a question to ask you."

"Ask."

"I know your boy mussed up my place the other night—"

"I specifically instructed him to be neat about it. I apologize."

"I accept the apology."

"That's what I like about you, Harry. You've always been a sensible man. Even when you were a cop, you kept your head."

"My place was mussed up again, only this time a very dear friend of mine happened to be there. He's now at Roosevelt Hospital looking like King Tut."

"I had nothing to do with it, Harry. My word on it."

"I figured you didn't, but sometimes I find it advisable to look past the obvious."

"It was not one of my boys."

"I'm sure you read about one of your boys being fished out of the East River."

"What a tragedy. It comes from free-lancing. Had Joe the Dude and Molloy played square with me, they would be alive now. I hasten to emphasize that I had nothing to do with the deaths of either of them. As I said the last time we talked, it appeared to me as if they had been doublecrossed by a third man."

"It was Joey Seldes, in case you didn't know or hadn't doped it out yourself."

"I confess that in my wildest dreams I would never have credited Joey with the brains or the guts to pull off something as grandiose as this Kipinski thing."

"As long as it's cards-on-the-table time, Mr. Madden, and before we resume our conversation about who may or may not have the diamonds, I'd like to know, just for my own satisfaction, when you found out about the Kipinski heist and came to the conclusion that three of your guys did it."

"I'm not a man who tells tales out of school, Harry."

"I know that, but it's no skin off your nose, is it? You weren't behind the heist. In a way, you were a victim, too. It's history."

Madden thought about it for a moment while he lit up a Spud, offered me one, shrugged when I declined in favor of a Lucky instead, and then, exhaling, said, "Okay. As you say, it's history, and I'm interested in establishing an atmosphere of trust and confidence between us before we discuss current events.

"It was two days after Christmas," he said, "and I was happily at ease down in Hot Springs. The last thing on my mind was the kind of business I used to be involved in before I went into retirement. Furthermore, it was Christmas week. I always made it a point to observe the Christian holidays. You can imagine my disgust and dismay when an associate called me long distance to inform me that there had been a very important heist and that two of my men had done it. I am not going to go into the details of how my associate knew. He knew. Okay?

"In that same call, I was told that Eddie Molloy had been found dead in a car over in Coney and that his partner in the crime, Joe the Dude Dennehy, probably had also been killed. My associate at that time did not know the identity of the killer, the person who inherited the Kipinski diamonds. It was a day or two before we learned that it was, *of all people,* Joey Seldes who had taken out Molloy and the Dude and inherited the stones. I suggested that my New York associates get in touch with Joey in an effort to obtain either an agreement to share the wealth, as Huey Long likes to say, or to lighten Joey's burdens.

"No, it was not my men who killed Joey that night at the Onyx. As I said, I have an aversion to business of that nature on the holidays. I instructed my associates to keep in touch with me and wait until the day after New Year's before dealing with Joey. In the interim, someone else killed him. I found that very frustrating, because Joey apparently died without telling anyone where he had put the gems. I did not know then, nor do I know at this moment, who iced Joey Seldes. At the first opportunity, I left my very pleasant surroundings in Hot Springs and returned to New York in the hope of coordinating a search for the legacy of the late Joseph Seldes. I arrived in town a couple of days ago. By that time, it was common knowledge that you were also looking into Joey's murder, and because I know you to be one of the finest detectives in this city, I assume you have located the diamonds or are close to locating them. Am I right?"

"If I had them, why would I still be working on this case?"

Madden made a face. "A good point. I assume, therefore, that the prospects of your locating the stones are good. For the same reason you suggest: you are still working on the case. I doubt if you'd be pursuing such a minor thing as Joey Seldes's death if you were not convinced that you would, sooner or later, learn his hiding place."

"That makes a lot of sense if you believe my only interest in the murder of Joey Seldes is the diamonds."

"What other reason is there?"

"Let's just say that I have a fondness for solving puzzles."

"You could buy the *Times* every day and do the crossword."

"I might only be interested in the cause of justice."

"You gave up that cause when you quit the police force." I let that crack hang in the air a moment. Madden took a puff from his Spud, blew a pair of smoke columns through his nostrils, and smiled the smuggest smile I'd ever had the distinct displeasure of witnessing. His Spud dangled from the corner of his lips.

I leaned toward him over the table. Like a Winchell tipster, I told him, "I want to say this very quietly, Mr. Madden. Okay?"

He leaned toward me, a hungry smile on his delicate lips, an eager glint in his eyes. A wisp of Spud smoke curled upward.

I whispered, *"Fuck . . . you."*

He reared back like a spooked horse. The Spud dropped from the corner of his mouth. "Nobody talks to me like that, MacNeil," he said flatly.

"I do, Owney! I do because I'm the guy who may know where the baubles are. I may know and you don't, and you want them and therefore I can say anything I want to you because you covet those diamonds more than you desire to settle any scores with me. So, I say it again, Owney the Killer: *Fuck you.*"

I half expected to become a Ben Turner by-line before I reached the exit, but I never looked back. I didn't hurry, and I showed no sign of how scared I was crossing the Terrace Court with my back turned toward a mobster whose reputation for viciousness was second only to Luciano's. The pair of gunsels who had issued my invitation to chat with Madden lurked on either side of the exit as I approached, but they never batted an eye as I walked between them. My pace was slow, measured. Until I was through that portal. Then I got my ass out of the Waldorf in a hurry. Snow never felt better as it cut into my face on a wind that howled along Park Avenue from the north. A Waldorf doorman smiled and tipped his hat and asked, "Cab, sir?" I gave a quick nod in reply and he blew his whistle. A Checker drew up, I climbed in, slapping a dollar bill into the doorman's gloved hand. "Thank you, sir!" he said, gently closing the door.

"Where to?" asked the cabbie.

"Anyplace but here," I said. "As fast as you can."

Two blocks away I told him to take me to Twenty-eighth and Broadway.

21

The Yorkville Stomp

The Lambda Society was open for business. Judging from the way the snow on the steps out front had been trod down, the Lambda Society was a thriving concern. Inside, the lobby's marble flooring was striped by wide rubber carpets. The whole place smelled of rubber, wet boots, and damp overcoats. In keeping with its Grecian exterior motif, the decor inside was all marble and pillars and classical statuary of muscular men, fauns, and Pans. It might have been a set for a Cecil B. DeMille epic except for a counter along one wall that had all the class of a Bowery hotel. Behind this long dark-wooded barrier, peering at me over the tops of his glasses, loitered the clerk of the curious establishment, a sallow young man with stringy brown hair and a bored manner. With all the answers on signs behind him for any question a customer might ask, the clerk of the establishment expected to have little to do except shuffle paper and collect the fees the signboards proclaimed in big black numbers. Nonetheless, the clerk asked, "May I help you?"

I walked over to the counter. "Is Kenny around?"

"Kenny who?"

"I was hoping you could tell me."

"I just rent the lockers, mister."

"Okay, rent me a locker. Next to Kenny's."

"I can live without the jokes, thanks."

"Do you know anyone named Kenny?"

"Everyone knows someone named Kenny."

Beginning to get a little irked, I said, still politely, "What do you say we start over? Pretend I just came in. You ask me, 'May I help you?' And I say, 'Is Kenny around?' "

"And I say, 'Kenny who?' "

"I could be wrong, but I don't think I am, so let's say for a moment that you do know Kenny and that you don't trust me for some reason, which leads me to think that Kenny is a fellow who might be a little astray of the law?"

"Are you the law?"

"Kind of."

"How can you be 'kind of' the law?"

"I'm a private investigator." I flashed my card. "I don't intend to bring any trouble down around Kenny's ears. I have to talk to him about a case, is all."

The clerk relaxed a little. He adjusted his eyeglasses and gave a little thought to what to say next. Finally, he said, "There are two Kenneths who are members of the Society."

"Pardon my ignorance, but what *is* the Lambda Society and what does membership get you?"

"It's a men's club. Membership gets you the use of the facilities—baths, steam room, masseur, a pool—and all the opportunities for socialization that go with being a member of a 'private' club."

"Is it a big membership?"

"Sizable."

"Oh. I gather that the exact details of club membership and who's a member would be confidential information?"

"Of course."

"Are you a member?"

The sallow youth flashed a smile. "I work here."

"Ah! I'll bet you're working nights and going to college days."

"Yes."

"City College?"

"Um-hm."

"I have a friend going there. Guy name of Joshua Sloman. Know him?"

"Thousands of students at City, mister."

"Sure. That's because it's *practically* free."

"There are . . . expenses." The clerk sighed, detecting a certain drift to our conversation.

"Books. Subways up and back. A date now and then. Adds up."

· "Rather quickly," he said.

I reached in my pocket and drew out a five-dollar note. "It would help me a lot to have a look at the membership list of this outfit."

"Yes, I'm sure it would," he said, a little nervously. It was clear that the five was tempting. I added two singles to it, keeping in mind what Lew Valentine had said about every man having a price and all you have to do is mention the right one. In the case of the clerk behind the desk in the drafty Cecil B. DeMille movie set, the price came to ten dollars. For the ten I got to look in the drawer he pulled from a wooden file box kept under the counter. There had to be a couple of hundred little cards with names on them. "You said there are two Kenneths?"

"Heywood and Kensington," he said.

Heywood, Kenneth, gave his address as Flushing, Queens. Kensington, Kenneth, listed his address as the Bronx. Beside each name was a number. "What's this?" I asked the clerk, tapping a fingernail against the digits.

"Locker number. Each member has a locker assigned the day he joins."

"How can you be sure these are real names?"

The kid turned over one of the cards to reveal a list of three names and addresses. "These are references. The first one is the sponsoring member. You must be sponsored to join the Lambda."

"Oh. That exclusive, hunh?"

"Well, it's a select club. Discretion is very important to the members."

"Why?" I asked. I paused a second before my second question. "Are the members queer?"

"I just assign the lockers, mister."

"I see," I said, sliding the cards of the two Kenneths back into the file. My fingers walked back through the stack to "S" and

flicked their way to the card for "Seldes, Joseph." Next to his
name was his date of membership, a year before, and his locker
number: 123. On the back were the requisite three names: Gary
Miller, sponsor; V. Dacapua, reference; Harry MacNeil, reference. Seeing my name gave me a chuckle. Next to it, handwritten,
was a notation, "Unable to contact H.M." I wondered what I
would have said if they'd actually reached me to solicit a personal reference for Joey. I slid the card back in place and took
out the card for "Miller, Gary. Address: 236 East 88th St.,
NYC." No phone listed. Locker No. 124. On the back of Gary
Miller's card were the required three names: Eric Lehman, Don-
ald Kempka, Walter Baur. "What can you tell me about Gary
Miller?"

The kid was beginning to tire of me and my questions and made
a face that gave expression to those feelings. "I could lose my
job, you know. So why don't you go away?"

"I'd like to have a look at locker number 123."

"Nope."

I shrugged. "Okay, then I'll just have to call the cops in on
this. I was hoping to avoid that, but . . ."

"No need for cops," he said urgently.

"Locker 123?"

"It's downstairs, but you'll have to go yourself, because I can't
leave the desk."

"Fair enough. Point me the way."

It was two flights down, each step leading me lower into the
stiflingly close and wet atmosphere of steam rooms and swim-
ming pools, soggy towels, athlete's foot baths, mildewed shower
stalls, and rows of green steel lockers. Row upon row of them
lined a room that smelled of socks and sweat. In a corner, I
found locker number 123.

It was unlocked. Open, it was empty.

"May I help you?"

I turned around to find a young man, naked to the towel
around his waist. His handsome face was ruddy from having just
come out of a shower. He looked at me suspiciously.

"Are you a new member?"

"Yes," I said, flashing a grin. "Well, actually, I'm thinking about joining. Giving the place the onceover, you know?"

The kid smiled and walked to his locker at the end of the row. "It's a friendly club."

"They said I could have number 123," I said, giving Joey Seldes's empty locker a thump with my fist.

"They emptied that one out a while ago."

"Ah! Did the man who had it quit the club?"

"I dunno. All I know is, one day last week, Kenny came in and broke the lock and cleaned out the stuff."

"Kenny?"

"The nigger porter."

Upstairs, the kid behind the desk was decidedly displeased to see me returning. An older man and a younger one were at the desk checking their valuables. (CHECK ALL VALUABLES, warned one of the placards behind the desk.) When the pair left and headed for the locker room, I crossed to the desk. "What happened to the stuff in number 123?"

"I beg pardon?"

"The locker, 123, that belongs to Joseph Seldes. It's empty. The lock's off. What happened to the stuff inside?"

I could see dawn breaking in the kid's mind. "Oh, sure! He's the guy that died. They cleaned out his locker."

"*Kenny* cleaned out the locker."

"Of course Kenny cleaned out ... ! *Kenny!*"

"Yeah! *Kenny!*"

"You know, I never even dreamed that you might mean *that* Kenny. He's the porter. Or, he *was* the porter until a few days ago."

"He's not the porter now?"

"He quit."

"When did Kenny quit?"

"Few days ago. Maybe a week."

"Or two, or three weeks ago?"

"Could be. I don't remember."

"What happened to the stuff from locker 123?"

"Stored."

"Where?"

"Here. Under the desk. We keep stuff from lockers that we have to break into. We keep it one month. That's a law, I think."

"You'd better let me see the stuff from 123."

"I don't know. I—"

"I don't want to hurt you, kid, and I ain't paying you any more money."

The goods from Joey Seldes's locker were in a laundry bag, tied and labeled with the number of his locker, as the kid dug under the counter and came up with it. From the bag I pulled an undershirt, sneakers, a pair of gym shorts, two pairs of stinking socks, a pair of khaki trousers, matching shirt, brown tie, patent-leather Sam Browne belt, brown boots, and a red armband with a white circle and a black swastika.

"Holy Christ," I muttered. "Joey Seldes was a fuckin' Nazi!"

"I beg your pardon?" asked the kid behind the counter.

"Nothing," I said, stuffing Joey's goods back into the sack.

"Is that everything you wanted, mister?"

"Not quite. I need to know Kenny-the-porter's address. Would you have that?"

Rolling back his eyes in exasperation, the kid opened a small telephone directory, looked up a name, and jotted the information on a scrap of paper: "Kendal Johnson, 250 West 134th Street."

"I'm taking these goods with me, kid," I announced, scooping up the address of Kendal Johnson with one hand and Joey Seldes's worldly possessions in the other.

"You can't!"

"Don't try to stop me, kid."

"Shit, I couldn't care less! Just so's you're leaving."

"I am, kid. Thanks. Good luck in college!"

There were no taxis to be had in the blizzard that seemed to be raging as I went outside, so I trudged through the snow to the Broadway subway, clutching Joey Seldes's goods as if they contained three million dollars in diamonds. They didn't, of course, which was both a puzzle and a disappointment. Everything I had learned and everything I now knew about the note Gloria had found among Joey's things pointed to the diamonds being in locker number 123. Because the gems were not among Joey's possessions taken from the locker, there were only two possibilities: the diamonds had not been in the locker at all, or, they had been hidden there and were now in the hands of the lucky gentleman who had had the task of cleaning out the locker.

I tried to imagine the look on Kendal Johnson's black face as he reached into the locker, pawing through the clothing, perhaps being as surprised as I at finding Joey's Nazi uniform, then gingerly taking hold of Joey's jockstrap (*the richest jock in town*) and discovering that it was stuffed with jewels.

No wonder Kendal Johnson quit his job, I thought as the uptown local clattered into the station. I boarded the last car and found only one other occupant. He looked up at me with passing interest, a gray-haired elderly black man who looked world weary in the extreme. I wondered if he was one of the millions of unemployed and then was sure he was and I wondered what a man like that would do if he stuck his hand in a locker and suddenly unearthed the wealth of the world at his fingertips. Even more interesting was to ask myself what a man like Kendal Johnson, who had a job, would do if he found a treasure. I was staring at the elderly Negro and he was starting to feel self-conscious. He was halfway down the car on the other side, glancing at me nervously while I stared at him and thought my thoughts about Kendal Johnson. Feeling a little stupid for having stared, I smiled and said, "It's a mean night out there tonight."

The Negro hesitated, then nodded. "Warm on the trains, though."

"Yeah, but soon your station comes, and you have to go up and out into the snow."

"I been ridin' this train all day."

"Ah, I think I understand."

"The wife expects I been lookin' for work. I gave up lookin' weeks ago. Months ago, now, I s'pose."

"I'm sorry, mister," I said.

"Ain't your fault. No cause for you to feel sorry. It's just the times."

"Life is unfair." I cracked a smile. "That's an old Irish saying. I'm Irish."

"That's a good, true sayin', mister."

"The Irish people have hard times, too."

"All peoples have hard times."

The train rumbled into the next station. The old Negro did not look up. It obviously didn't matter what station it was. A woman in a snow-flecked brown coat got on and sat at the far end of the car.

"Times will get better," said the old man as the train moved again. "Roosevelt is a fine man. Roosevelt will turn the country around."

"What would you do if you suddenly struck it rich, mister?"

The old man chuckled. "Pinch myself to see if I woke up. I s'pose I would wake up, too." He giggled at his joke on himself.

"If you had a job and you really struck it rich . . ."

"You mean if I hit the right number in the policy game?"

"Like that, yeah."

"Oh, I s'pose I'd spend a little havin' a nice time but most of it I'd spend on the wife and kids."

"Would you quit your job?"

"If you'd a ast me that question when I had a job, I would a said I'd quit like that." He snapped his fingers. "Only I ain't got a job, an' if I gets one I won't quit it very quick even if I would hit the policy jackpot."

The train arrived at my stop and I got up to leave. The old man watched me as far as the door and I half expected him to ask me if I could spare a dime, but he just turned down his head and stared at the floor as I stepped off the train and the doors slid closed. I wondered if I should have offered him a couple of bucks, but I told myself that the old man would have turned it down flat, which is what I was sure he would have done.

I found a phone booth and called Ben Turner at the *News*. "Ben, can you get away a couple of minutes and meet me at that greasy spoon across the street? In fifteen minutes?"

I was there in ten. Ben was there in twenty. The paint remover coffee was before us a minute later. "What's up?"

"I have two places to visit tonight and in this foul weather it would sure help if I had a car."

"You wish me to wangle a *News* car?"

"There's an address in Harlem I have to find, but first I want to stop off at another address."

"What's up, Harry? I've never seen you so keyed up, and I've seen you on a lot of cases."

"I was damned sure I'd have the Kipinski diamonds tonight."

"Holy cow!"

"Only they weren't where I thought they'd be. I have a feeling they *had* been there. Everything pointed to it. Trouble is, I don't know if Joey moved them or somebody found them through a stroke of pure dumb luck."

For Ben's edification, I went over the case, leading him along all the twisting paths I'd followed, right up to my visit to the Lambda Society and going downstairs to locate Joey's locker. "Yeah"—Ben nodded—"I'd've expected to find Joey's little treasure trove myself."

"This is what I found." Dumping Joey's bag of clothing onto the table and nearly burying the cups of paint remover, I picked through the items and unfolded before the Jew Benjamin Turner's eyes the red-white-and-black Nazi armband. "How do you add that up, hunh, Ben?"

"I add it up to a sick mind and a soul as twisted as that black cross."

"If I were a fancy Park Avenue psychiatrist at fifty bucks an hour, I'd say that Joseph Seldes was suffering from delusions of grandeur."

"There's no grandeur in that rag," said Ben, nodding toward the armband.

"It proves that Joey was in the process of switching his allegiance from the Madden gang to this one."

"On top of everything else that creep was, he was a traitor."

"Ambition is a terrible thing, Ben."

"What are you doin' about this?"

"I should first have a talk with the ape who appears to have recruited Joey into the Nazis. His name is Gary Miller and he lives up on Eighty-eighth Street."

"Yorkville." Ben nodded.

"Yup," I said. "Germantown."

Ben broodingly slurped his coffee.

"That's why I thought, if you could get a car—"

"We'll go across to the city room and I'll *get* a car."

Efforts to bring out the next edition of the *Daily News* were in full stride as we walked across the city room. I waited at Ben's desk while he had a chat with his boss. He came back a minute later, saying it was okay to have the car. "I told him it would be a big story when I had it all together. I hope it is, Harry."

"I appreciate your being my chauffeur, Ben."

"I'm going in with you, no matter what you find up there in Yorkville, Harry."

"You know what I'm likely to find."

"A nest of Nazis."

"Ratzis, as Winchell calls 'em."

"Well, I guess I have to agree with Walter on that one."

"Ben, you stay in the car. This is no job for a little Jewish guy with no hair, no wind, and no idea whatsoever about how to handle himself if it comes to a scrap with a street-bully Nazi."

"Are you going to beat the shit out of this Miller character if he doesn't cooperate?"

"It's possible."

"Then I'm going."

"Ben, it doesn't concern you."

"Standing up to the Nazis doesn't concern me? I'm a Jew, Harry. If it doesn't concern me, who does it concern?"

"It'll be rough, probably."

"I hope so. I pray to Jehovah it will get rough."

With that, he reached into his desk and pulled out the biggest, meanest sap I'd ever laid eyes on.

The address of Gary Miller was on the south side of Eighty-eighth Street, near Second Avenue, almost at the bottom of the hill which Eighty-eighth Street is at that point. The building was a brownstone apartment house, the reddish brown facade flecked with wind-blown snow. Piles of snow looked like pillows on the steps going up to the door. In the lobby, I scanned the names on the mailboxes and found one with two names on it: "G. Miller" and "Gerhardt Mueller, Gauleiter, G. A. Bund, Yorkville Battalion." It was all I could do to keep Ben from kicking it down when we found the vestibule door locked. "What now?" muttered Ben. "You gonna pick it?"

Pressing the button next to Miller-Mueller's name, I waited for a reply on the intercom. "Yes?" came a young man's voice.

Ben and I exchanged looks, then I said into the intercom, "Heil Hitler!"

"Who is it?" the voice came back.

"I was told by a friend at the Lambda to see you about joining your group."

After a long pause, the voice on the intercom asked, "Who at the Lambda?"

I gulped air and said, "Joey Seldes."

"Joey is dead."

I waited a moment, wondering what to do, what to say. What I said was "I came about the Kipinski diamonds."

"Jesus," groaned Ben behind me.

A second later, the vestibule door buzzed open.

Ben and I went up slowly to a third-floor apartment. Finding the right one was easy. A swastika decorated it. I knocked.

Gary—Gerhardt Mueller—Miller opened his apartment door just far enough to make it easy for me to push it all the way open and to send him staggering backwards into his room. Ben and I barged in. Steadying himself, Gary Miller was exactly as Vito Dacapua had described him—a blond Adonis, all muscle and good looks and all-American clean-cut from head to foot, except for his brown shirt, his leather belt, the khaki riding breeches, the knee-high boots, and the Nazi armband. "Who are you? What is this?" he demanded.

"Sit down, Herr Gerhardt," I snapped. "We're gonna have a talk about our mutual friend."

"I doubt if we have any mutual friends. Not if your friends are like him."

I had to hold Ben back. "I'm talking about Joey Seldes," I said. Ben relaxed.

"Seldes is dead. A common criminal."

"Like the rest of you bastards," commented Ben from behind me.

"I have nothing to do with Seldes. Not any more," said Gerhardt Mueller disdainfully.

"Is that because Joey disappointed you by getting killed before he could hand over the Kipinski diamonds?"

The Nazi grunted a laugh. "He never had them."

I shook my head. "Not true. He had them."

"It was all talk."

"But true talk. You should have had more respect for Joey. We all should have had more respect for Joey."

The Nazi smiled. "Perhaps. Do you know where the diamonds are?"

"They're not on me. I can tell you that."

"I assumed not."

"What were you going to do with the gems, Gary?"

"My name is Gerhardt. I have given up the anglicized name."

"Gerhardt Schmerhardt," said Ben, getting antsy again behind me.

"Your Jew friend wants to make trouble." The Nazi smirked.

"Yes, he does."

"And you?"

"Me? I want to make talk."

"I have nothing to say."

"I think you will," I said quietly. I slipped my .38 from under my shoulder to underscore the words.

The Nazi shrugged, eased back a pace, and sat on a wooden chair beside his paper-cluttered desk. Above the desk a pair of crossed swastika flags made an arch over a framed portrait of der Führer, Herr Hitler himself. "You said from downstairs that you wished to discuss the diamonds. You lied."

"Look who's complaining about lying," cracked Ben.

"The Jew behind you makes tough talk, but I notice he stays behind you." The Nazi laughed.

Ben bolted away from me, dashing across the room and onto the Nazi before I knew what was happening. By the time I pulled Ben away, he'd let the Nazi have two or three whacks with his sap. The Nazi slumped to the floor as Ben reluctantly stepped back from him. "Sit down, Ben and cool off," I shouted. Ben backed off. I bent over the Nazi, carefully keeping my gun out of his reach.

"Be careful of that louse, Harry," Ben warned.

The Nazi was bleeding at the hairline in front of his left ear but seemed otherwise okay. Recovering from the stunning blows, he stirred and sat up straight. "You see who is the first to resort to violence. The Jew. Always the Jew."

"Just shut the hell up, Nazi!" I said. "Shut up about the Jews or I might just decide to let Ben do what he'd like to do. It might even be fun to watch."

"If you didn't come here to beat me up," the Nazi asked, "why did you come?"

I backed away and uncoiled a bit. I kept my .38 pointed in the Nazi's direction. "I've been down a long and twisting trail these couple of days, and I'm fed up with it. I want to know *now* all about Joey Seldes and how he got hooked into Nazis and why; and I have to warn you, Herr Gerhardt, that if you don't level with me I might blow your fuckin' head off just for the pleasure of it."

The Nazi mulled my words over and began to talk.

"Joey and I met at a meeting over a year ago. It was a political gathering where I was the speaker. The subject was National Socialism and how it applied to America, how National Socialism is the answer to the Depression and decadent capitalism, not the sick Jew-ridden program of Franklin Roosevelt's New Deal.

"I frankly was surprised that Joey was interested in politics. Then I realized that he was more interested in the young man who had brought him to the meeting. I later heard tales about Joey being a mobster. He was a misfit in the mob, I was told, but it is my belief that the American Nazi movement must take root among all those who either are misfits or who believe they are. Revolutions may be led by thinkers such as myself and Hitler, but the muscle, the force, comes from men like Joey.

"We talked on a number of occasions. I discovered that he was quite interested in me personally. I found a certain fascinating quality in him. Joey was notorious in some circles in which I traveled as well. We became quite close to each other. I arranged for him to become a member of the Lambda Society. Many of our movement's members belong. It provides a convenient and discreet place to meet.

"It was at one of our meetings near the end of last year that Joey came to me and told me that he could provide a very large amount of money to finance our operations. I pressed him on this and he told me that he had learned of a theft that was being planned by two members of his gang. Diamonds. Millions of dollars' worth of diamonds. He asked me, quite bluntly, what he would get out of it by delivering such a prize to the movement's coffers. I told him he would achieve a very high rank. I promised him that at the moment of the success of the revolution he would be an important member of the party here in New York. He was quite pleased at the prospect and he told me that he would deliver the diamonds to me in a few days. I did not really believe him, of course. Then I read in the newspapers of the disappearance of the Jew gem merchant, and I knew that Joey had not been lying to me. He phoned early on New Year's Eve and promised me that the next day he would bring me the diamonds. As you know, he was murdered that very evening. I never saw the diamonds."

The Nazi smiled. "Am I to understand that you know where they are?"

"I know where they *were*."

"Of what interest is it to me where they were?"

"It's just ironic, is all."

"Save the irony, sir."

"They were in locker 123 at the Lambda all along. You had 124, I believe?"

"The locker next to mine?"

"Yeah. From what I've been able to figure, he kept them there in a jockstrap. He called it 'the richest jock in town.' Of course, as you know, they emptied Joey's locker out after he was killed. His Nazi duds were there, but no jockstrap. All the time, they were next to your locker. Right under your nose. It's a wonder you didn't smell 'em."

The Nazi laughed. "Perhaps if I'd had a Jew nose like your friend's—"

Ben was on him in a flash, leaping almost halfway across the room, slamming into him like a Notre Dame tackle, thumping to the floor with the Nazi, splintering the chair. For a moment, Ben was doing very well, but the Nazi was younger and stronger, and it was only a second before he flipped Ben onto his back. The Nazi sat astride him like a horse. In his hand, raised over Ben's head, he waved a broken chair leg, its ragged, splintered point as sharp and lethal-looking as any barroom dagger I'd ever seen.

"Filthy Jew swine!" the Nazi screamed.

The arm plunged.

It never found its target.

A slug from my .38 blew the Nazi off Benny, halfway across the room, and slam up against a wall.

He was dead in mid-flight, drilled through the right temple.

Police Comissioner Lewis J. Valentine was always described by newspaper guys like Ben Turner as "gruff," and Lew was that. Chin like a rock. Piercing blue eyes. Tall—so tall he would tower over La Guardia when they had reason to be side by side. He had the hardness that comes from being a beat cop. He'd risen through the ranks to become an inspector but was busted to precinct captain on the other side of the East River, an exile of six years, because Tammany Hall bosses didn't cotton to his raids on political clubhouses. Shortly after La Guardia took office, Valentine was rescued from oblivion and quickly put in command of the New York Police Department. We were old friends.

"Harry," he said as I was ushered into his office on Centre Street, "I want you to explain to me what the hell is going on. Why have my men brought you in on a murder charge—Harry MacNeil, an old friend and a great cop—and the murder turns out to be the shooting of a goddamned punk with ideas that he's the Hitler of Yorkville?"

"Can I sit?" I asked.

"Sure you can sit. Lay down on the floor. I don't care. Just tell me what the hell's going on."

"Can I ask you one question first, Lew? I mean, Commissioner?"

"It's Lew and ask your question already."

"How did your boys get there so fast? No sooner did I

splatter that Nazi son of a bitch, and your boys were all over me."

"I'll give you the answer to that after you tell me your tale of woe, Harry."

"I've broken the Kipinski diamond case, for starters."

Valentine whistled through his teeth, rocked slowly back in his chair, and folded his hands across his belly. "I was told that case was at a dead end. More so after they fished that body out of the water the other day."

"The heist was pulled by Eddie Two Fingers Molloy and Joe the Dude Dennehy. They free-lanced it. Owney Madden had no part in it. In fact, he's damned perturbed to have been left out in the cold. He's back in town, you know."

"At the Waldorf." Valentine nodded.

"He thinks I have the gems."

"Do you?"

"Not yet."

"Go on."

"There was a third partner in the Kipinski kidnapping and robbery: Joey Seldes, a hanger-on with the Madden mob."

"He was murdered a few weeks back?"

"He was gunned down at the Onyx Club on New Year's Eve."

"I recall it now. Inspector Grady handled the investigation."

"Right."

He remembered from the way I replied how I felt about Grady. "You two still don't like each other, I see."

"He's been on my tail. Do you know anything about that, Lew?"

"No, but knowing Grady, he must have his reasons."

"Well, I'm gonna find out what they are."

"You're in enough trouble, Harry. Forget Grady. I want to know about the Kipinski case and, if you ever get around to it, why you shot that Nazi uptown tonight."

"It's all one big ball of wax, Lew."

"I'm listening."

"Seldes was the third man in the Kipinski heist, as I said. Only he proved a lot smarter than the other two. Joey killed them. I have the gun. Your ballistics men will be able to match the bullets taken from Dennehy and Molloy. I said, 'I have the gun.' Actually, your men who arrested me have it. They confiscated it along with mine tonight up on Eighty-eighth Street. Anyway, Joey Seldes bumped off his pals and wound up with all the diamonds. He stashed them in a locker at a place called the Lambda Society. Seems to be a queer hangout up on Twenty-eighth."

"I know about the place," said the Police Commissioner, rocking a little in his big chair, his icewater eyes on me.

"The gems aren't there anymore. I'm sure they were. Sometime after Joey was rubbed out, the Lambda club cleaned the locker out to rent it again. You see, Joey was killed before he had a chance to make his big play with the diamonds."

"What big play?"

"This is the amazing part, Lew! Joey was on his way toward becoming a Nazi."

"At last I see the connection!"

"Joey planned to use the diamonds—most of 'em, that is—to buy himself a high-ranking spot in the Nazi hierarchy. He planned to keep plenty of the stones for his own use, of course, mainly to finance a lot of world traveling with his boyfriend."

"*Boy*friend?"

"A kid named Vito Dacapua, brother of the gunsel in the Luciano outfit. The kid's a fairy, and Joey was a switch hitter when it suited him. Only the kid's brother was not at all happy about Joey messing around with the kid. He'd warned him, I gather, and when Joey didn't lay off, the older Dacapua sent a pair of torpedoes up to the Onyx that night to get rid of the little pest permanently. You'll want to pick up Vito Dacapua and his brother. Lean on little Vito. He resents his brother a lot. You'll sew up the rubout of Joey Seldes quite nicely, plus the Kipinski case."

"Except for the diamonds."

"Yeah."

"But you're not going to tell me where they are!"

"No, I'm not."

Police Commissioner Lewis Valentine ceased his gentle rocking

and sat up straight behind his desk. "Harry, you were picked up
on a homicide charge. Withholding evidence as to the diamonds
is obstruction of justice, in addition."

"I had to shoot that Nazi creep. He was about to kill Ben
Turner, who will testify to it. You could try for an indictment,
but you won't get it. I'm not worried about any homicide charge."

"I can hold you until you tell us where the diamonds are."

"I won't. You know I won't. The longer you hold me, the better
the chances the diamonds will never be recovered."

"I'm supposed to turn you loose so you can go and look for
the diamonds?"

"Yep."

"A man could travel far if he found all that ice."

"Very far."

"What guarantee do I have that you won't leave town?"

"The guarantee of knowing me and my record as a cop. The
guarantee of the friendship we've had over a lot of years. The
guarantee of knowing that Harry MacNeil not in New York City
is Harry MacNeil out of his element. When you leave New York,
you don't go anywhere, even with three million in diamonds in
your pocket. Besides, do you know any place in the world where
I can hear good jazz like I can hear every night up on The
Street?"

"I'd have to call the District Attorney before I let you go."

"There's the phone."

He rocked again, thinking, then picked up the phone and dialed.
"You're a character, Harry! Always were."

"They're holding Ben Turner downstairs. Ben gets sprung, too.
He's a victim, if he's anything."

On the phone, the Police Commissioner told the other party
who he was and why he was calling. He waited for the D.A. to
come on the line. "You've told me everything but how you got
into this in the first place."

"I've got a client." I smiled.

"A dame?"

"Naturally."

The gist of what Valentine said to the D.A. was that he in-

tended to turn Mr. MacNeil loose because there was not really
enough evidence to hold him. He was telling the D.A., not asking,
although he was far more polite than I might have been if the
situation were reversed. The discussion lasted about five minutes,
after which he put down the phone and smiled. "You're sprung.
There'll have to be a formal hearing someday. You know how
D.A.'s are! Ben is sprung, too. He'll have to be a witness at the
hearing. I'm out on the limb on this, Harry."

"Now you have to answer my question."

Valentine chuckled. "I'll let someone else give you the answer.
He'll be very interested in your story. As it happens, your arrest
has made me late for an appointment with the man, so come on,
Harry, we're going uptown."

"I'd like Ben to come along. He's been with me throughout.
For him, it'll be a big story for his paper."

"We'll gather Ben into our fold on the way out the door."

In the back of Valentine's Cadillac, Ben Turner and the Commissioner renewed old times after Valentine broke the pleasant
news that Ben and I were no longer under arrest, a statement
that relieved Ben a great deal, he said, adding with his usual flair
for poking a toe at sleeping dogs, "However, I was looking
forward to getting the direct personal proof that you cops have
a special room at headquarters where they break out the rubber
hoses."

Valentine laughed as he said, "You'd've been disappointed,
Ben. The Mayor's cut our budget for rubber hoses this year."

At 1274 Fifth Avenue, the Cadillac glided noiselessly to the
curb. The new snow was already an extra inch added to the four
of a couple of days before and still coming down. The sidewalk
was swept, however, as were the steps leading into the tenement-
style building where Fiorello H. La Guardia had lived for years.
The cleaned pavement and the uniformed policeman at the door
provided the only evidence that the Mayor of New York lived
inside.

His pert and pretty wife, Marie, opened the apartment door, loosing from inside the apartment a breeze laden with the delicious smell of Italian cooking. A moment later, a short, chubby, improbable figure emerged through the kitchen door. A stovepipe chef's hat was perched atop the round head, the black hair coiling out from under it. In his hand, the Mayor clutched a large wooden spoon. An apron draped his bulging belly. On the apron hung a row of La Guardia's medals from the war. In his falsetto voice, he shouted down the hallway from the kitchen door, "Lew, you are late! Any later and the dinner would've been ruint. Who's that with you?"

Valentine did the introductions, and I was pleased to learn that La Guardia remembered my name. "You're MacNeil, the famous unpolitical flatfoot." The Mayor chuckled. "Oh, I heard about your interview with Mayor Walker. Jimmy got a kick out of telling that story. And Benjamin Turner of the *News*. Is this visit on the record?"

"Not at all, Mr. Mayor." Ben blushed.

"Too bad!" exclaimed La Guardia. "It would do your readers good to know that their Mayor's not to proud to do a little kitchen work. Excuse the costume. It's customary when I cook for guests."

"An impressive array of medals, Mr. Mayor," replied Ben.

La Guardia beamed. "Yes. What did you do in the war, Mr. Turner?"

"*Stars and Stripes.*"

"Ah, a fine newspaper. I never missed it. You know Franklin P. Adams and Alec Woollcott and the rest."

"I surely do, Mr. Mayor."

"Say, I hope you two are staying for dinner!"

"It'd be a pleasure." Ben beamed.

"Delighted," said I. "Considering that half an hour ago I was expecting to eat dinner in a New York City jail!"

"Ah, now that sounds like a story fit to be told over my lasagne." La Guardia laughed. "Leave it to Lew Valentine to brighten up the evening by bringing along a pair of fascinating guests. Make yourselves at home. Marie! Take their coats and see that they're comfortable while I complete my kitchen magic act."

La Guardia barely touched his delicious meal as I related all I had learned of the curious circumstances and effects of the rubout of Joey Seldes. He grew especially attentive as I came to the part about Gerhardt Mueller and how and why I had to blow his brains out only a few hours earlier. The Mayor's wife listened with all the stoicism of a woman grown accustomed to the horror stories of the worlds of politics and police. She served coffee and Italian ice cream while I wound up the story, affixing to my narrative the question I'd asked Lew Valentine and which he had promised an answer for.

La Guardia pushed his chair back a little and lit up a cigar. "We've had that tinhorn Nazi's house under surveillance a long time," he said, dragging out the "a" in Nazi and turning the word into an epithet. He puffed his cigar like a Pennsy locomotive getting up steam for a steep climb. "The Nazis are just another gang to me. No better than Luciano's monkeys. Or Owney Madden's. In most ways, the Nazis are worse. Tinhorns and chiselers! I'm not going to let them get their greasy paws on this town! The ugly part is, this Mueller and his followers are *Americans!* If they were from Germany, I'd've given 'em the boot long ago. Run 'em out of town, that's what I'd've done. I couldn't do that, so I told Lew Valentine to keep an eye on them. He set up a special detail months ago. I guess it was the boys on the detail who were so quick to respond when they heard the shot in Mueller's apartment. I'm against killing of any kind, but I can't tell you that I'm sorry that tinhorn is out of our hair."

Suddenly the Mayor stood up and went over to a chair to fetch a thick black leather briefcase. He came back to the table, sat, and plopped the case on his lap. Rummaging through it, he produced a letter which he laid on the table until he could reach under his jacket to fish out his reading glasses.

"Now, this is a letter from Herr von Ribbentrop himself. He's the Nazi Foreign Minister, in case you're not up on these things. In this letter, he lodges a protest with me against some of the things I've said in public about the character of Herr Hitler and his gang over in Berlin and his American toadies over here. Then Herr von Ribbentrop goes on to relate that an emissary of the Foreign Ministry is coming over on business and will be staying at the German consulate. In this next sentence, he expresses concern that, quote, American Jews may try to make trouble, unquote. He *demands* extra police protection!"

The Mayor folded the letter and shoved it into his briefcase, which he put on the floor by his foot. He took off his spectacles and tucked them away.

"Well," he said, clasping his hands prayerlike as he propped his elbows on the table, "I'm ordering them *plenty* of protection. Lew is calling in the police duty rosters and picking out the finest men on the force." The Mayor paused and sank back in his chair, letting his hands drop into his lap. "Jews, every one of them!"

Ben Turner laughed no harder than the Mayor.

"You would not believe," said the Mayor, suddenly somber and frowning, "how much these Nazis have grown over here! I heard from a city official in Yaphank out on Long Island that a developer wants to establish what he calls 'German Gardens' in that town. It will boast street names such as Adolf Hitler Strasse! Göring Strasse! Goebbels Strasse! Can you picture Hitler's swastika flag flying over a piece of Long Island?"

The Mayor's face was flushed and his hand trembled slightly with anger as he reached for a handkerchief to blot a veneer of perspiration from his brow. His eyes skipped from face to face around the table.

"To me, these Nazis are just another underworld gang of racketeers and killers, and the sooner the American people wake up to that fact the better off we'll all be."

He stared at me with unflinching eyes.

"Harry, they must not get their hands on those diamonds. I don't know about Lew Valentine's strategy in leaving it up to you to retrieve them. I know that Lew Valentine is a great Commissioner whose judgments have been excellent. I can only stress that I'm counting on you, Harry, as much as Lew is."

He tucked his handkerchief back into his breast pocket and smiled. "Now, tell me. How do you like the spumoni?"

"It's delicious, Mr. Mayor."

He smiled like a cherub as he anticipated my question. "No, I didn't make it. It's store-bought!"

When it was time to leave, La Guardia went down to the street with us and shook hands with Ben and me.

To Lew Valentine he said, "I'm not happy about Owney Madden being back in town. Deliver him a message from me, Lewis. Send a couple of your best men around—or go yourself, if you wish—and inform that gangster I want his ass out of my city by sunup."

As I climbed into the back of the Commissioner's Cadillac, La Guardia waved and shouted, "Patience and fortitude, Harry!"

23

The Music Goes Round & Round

The Department of Streets was having a hard time keeping pace with the snow. Fifth Avenue was fine, but the crosstown streets were deepening with it, so I suggested to Lew Valentine that his driver could let me out at the corner of Fifty-second rather than going out of the way on such a blustery and snowy night. Ben chose to ride with the Commissioner as far as Forty-second, then to hike to the *News* to write a story that was going to cause the editors to remake the front page. "Nothing about the diamonds, Ben," I cautioned him.

"Not yet, Harry." Ben frowned. "That story's gonna be my Pulitzer."

The snow gave them most of Fifth Avenue to themselves as the Cadillac crept away.

I'd decided that it was much too late and too snowy to go up to Harlem in search of Kendal Johnson, but I was also beginning to come to terms with the ugly fact that I'd shot a human being to death in the shank of this white, peaceful, cold, and cleansing February night. Being arrested, the chat with Valentine, and dinner with La Guardia had bound my nerves together like baling wire for hours, but as I walked and slipped on the snows of The Street, I felt them starting to come apart. At the very least, I needed a drink. The inviting lights of a big sign spelling out O N Y X blazed through the swirling snow.

Four drinks, four flights up, and twelve hours later, I woke up to the smell of perfume that had to have come from Saks. I

opened my eyes on the couch and saw her standing by my desk
in the same fur coat she'd been wearing the day she hired me.
The hat could have been the same. All her hats looked alike,
cocked to the right over her eye. She was taking a drag on a
Marlboro. "Well, good morning, sleepyhead!"

"Is it? What the hell are you doing here? What time's it?"

"About four P.M."

"It's too early to get up."

"You were all over the newspaper this morning." She held up
the front page of the *News*.

I had to blink my eyes a couple of times to see clearly, even a
headline as big as the one in the paper:

PRIVATE EYE

KILLS N.Y.C.

NAZI FÜHRER

"Sweet and succinct." I groaned, getting up.

"I saw it and feared it was you," she said, folding the paper and
dropping it on my desk. "I was awfully scared, almost too scared
to read it. I thought you were in jail. I thought I'd never see you
again."

I went over to the desk and opened the drawer where the scotch
was. I poured two glasses of it, but she didn't take hers. "Here's
to habeas corpus," I said, downing the whiskey.

"Habeas . . .?

"Latin. Means, 'Where is the body?' Or something like that.
In law, it means that in the United States of America, if a fellow
is arrested for killing someone, you can't lock him up and throw
away the key without due process. In short, it means if you've
got a good lawyer or a good excuse, you can get sprung. I was
sprung."

"I'm glad, Harry."

"What made you sure it was me when you saw the headline?"

"I don't know. I had a feeling. It's the kind of thing you'd do.
It said you came to the aid of a Jew who was about to be as-
saulted by this Nazi."

"It was almost like that."

"So like you. Sir Galahad."

I wanted coffee but I had another scotch because I had scotch and didn't have coffee. "Did you know about Joey being a Nazi!"

"A Nazi? Joey?"

"A Nazi. Joey."

"Don't be ridiculous."

"I warned you about telling another lie to me, honey."

"Why should I know about Joey being a Nazi? If he was one, I mean."

"Because Joey told you everything. He did, didn't he?"

"He didn't tell me where the diamonds are."

I laughed.

"He never told me about his boyfriends, either."

"Well, I can see how he might not tell you about his fairy friends, but being a Nazi was just too big a deal in Joey's bent-out-of-shape life not to tell the gal he loved and really wanted to impress."

"Joey being a Nazi would not have impressed me."

"Did you tell him that you weren't impressed?"

"I told you, I never talked with him about his being a Nazi."

"Yeah, you told me."

Suddenly she sat, letting her fur open a bit and her legs show, like the day she hired me. She looked at me cockeyed again, like that day. She patted her hairdo, still rusty-red. "Have you found the diamonds?"

"Do you suppose the gems were at that Nazi's place?"

"Why else would you go there?"

"It's interesting how you don't care all that much anymore about bringing Joey's killers to justice. All you care about is the goods Joey seems to have collected in his last couple of days on earth."

"When I came to see you about hiring you, I didn't know Joey had any diamonds."

"Oh, of course you knew, darling. The note. That newspaper article. Joey's big talk about having a second honeymoon. You had to know he had the Kipinski gems. Maybe he even told you he had them."

"He didn't tell me anything about any diamonds, Harry."

"Maybe not. Else why hire me to find out if he'd had them?"

"What's wrong with that?"

"Nothing, except you could have been a little more straight-forward about why you came here a couple of days ago with your widow's tears and the little catch in your voice while you pleaded with me to obtain justice for your late husband."

"Well, I hardly knew you then."

"True. We know each other better now, though."

"I was also quite afraid for my own life that day."

"Afraid for your own life? How come?"

"I was afraid that if Joey'd had the diamonds, the men he worked with would come looking for them."

"Oh, they'd've done that long before you came round to me, darling."

"I had no way of knowing that."

"I suppose not."

"It seemed to me that if you found out who killed Joey, I wouldn't have to worry about them coming around. That's one reason I moved. I didn't want anyone who knew where Joey lived to come around where I was living. I was scared, Harry. Really scared."

"But it was okay if along the way to finding out who killed Joey I also stumbled onto where Joey'd hidden the gems.

"Have you found out?"

"I have found out a lot of things on this case. Seems every turn of a corner brought a new revelation. Joey being queer for that Dago kid. The kid was full of surprises himself. Plus this Nazi thing. That one really knocked me for a loop. A couple of bodies showed up, too. Joe the Dude, blown up like a balloon after a couple of weeks in the East River! A dead Nazi, his head blown off by a gun in my hand. *Twice* my pretty little office got turned inside out. First time by Madden's boy. The second time by someone who took a great deal of delight in messing up a good friend of mine, who may die because of it. Since the day you walked in that door, darling, my life has not exactly been a bowl of cherries."

"Have you located the diamonds?" she asked again, quite coolly.

"I found out who killed your husband, which is what you paid me for. It was a couple of hired guns. The big brother of that little Wop lover of your husband's ordered Joey rubbed out. Only that doesn't interest you, I see. No. You just care about the diamonds. You have a one-track mind, Gloria, darling."

"All right, I am thinking about the diamonds. I was thinking about them—and wanting them—when I hired you."

"Now we're getting somewhere," I said, pulling out my desk chair with the toe of my shoe and sitting down to lean back, nurse my scotch, and listen.

"Of course I knew about the diamonds! I knew about them on the day they were stolen from that merchant. Joey told me everything. He came home that night more excited than ever before. He could barely contain himself, although at first he wouldn't tell me what he was so pleased about. I tried to wangle it out of him, but he just told me to sit tight and in a few days he and I would be able to have the big honeymoon we'd never had. He said he was going to be very rich and very important and that I would soon learn what a great man he was.

"I tried and tried to get him to tell me more, but he kept saying, 'No, you gotta wait on this one. You'll know when it's the right time.' He was so high from whatever it was he'd done that I knew I wouldn't get anything out of him just by asking. So I started playing up to him, telling him that his excitement was getting me very excited, and that if this was as big a day as he said it was, we should celebrate it together, in the way he and I could celebrate so well. He was always easy to flatter. All I ever had to do was make him think that nothing pleased me more than to be in bed with him. Then I could always get Joey to do or say anything I wanted him to do or say.

"It wasn't long before he told me everything about the caper he'd pulled off. He said he'd been taken for a sucker by Molloy and Dennehy. He'd helped them plan and stage the kidnapping. He said without him in the scheme it never would have worked. He said he was the one who was going to turn the diamonds into cash, but once the two of them had the stones, they planned to turn on Joey. They had planned all along to kill him, he said. Of course, he suspected them and was ready for them. Instead of them killing him, he killed them. He said he'd put the diamonds in a very safe place where only he would know where they were.

"He was proud of being so smart, but I asked him what would happen if he couldn't get to the diamonds. What if something went wrong and he was picked up by the cops? What if someone accidentally found the diamonds while he was laying low? I told him he ought to tell me where they were, just in case. He said I was being a dumb broad. He asked me what would keep me from trying to get the diamonds myself and leaving him holding the bag? I told him I wouldn't do that, because I loved him. He laughed at that. He had a really good laugh. Nothing I could do could get him to tell me where he'd put the diamonds. He said it was only a few days, anyway. He was going to make the deal on New Year's Day. He said he would have money, not gems, on New Year's Day. You know what happened New Year's Eve."

"How do you account for the note you found in that pocket?" I asked.

She decided to have the scotch that sat in front of her on the corner of the desk. She sipped it daintily and made a face. "Warm! Needs ice."

"How do you account for the note?"

"I can only guess. What I guess is, he started worrying about what I'd said about something happening to him, so he wrote out that note."

"Why in code?"

"I don't know," she said, looking at me angrily.

"I figure he wrote it for someone who knew about the diamonds and would know what the code meant."

"He never told anyone else about the diamonds."

"Darling, you know he told Vito Dacapua about them. He even gave him one. He told his Nazi pal, too. What's more, and I'm sorry if this hurts your feelings, darling, he also promised to share the payoff from the diamonds with his fairy lover and his jackbooted pal up in Yorkville. Your husband was a very generous fellow. The only question is, which of you three did he intend to give that note to?"

"We'll probably never know."

"Maybe not, although you can make yourself feel better about him if you let yourself believe that he wrote the note and put it in that coat pocket expecting that one day *you'd* find it."

"But how would I know what it meant?"

"Oh, that'd be easy." I smiled. "You'd hire a detective to figure it out for you."

"Yes. He knew I'd hire you if it came to that. *That's* why he came to see you that night at the Onyx. To tell you that I might come to you for help someday." She smiled and gulped scotch and smiled again. "Joey was very smart to think it through like that, wasn't he?"

"Yeah, *if* he came to see me and for that reason."

"It must have been the reason."

"*If* he came looking for me, that'd be as good a reason as any, only Joey never came looking for me that night, darling."

"Oh, but he did. He told me—"

"Uh, uh."

"He did. He—"

"That was one of your lies along the way, and like the others, I was suckered into it."

"Others?"

"One, your not knowing the Dago kid."

"I explained that."

"Yes, you did, but I didn't believe you. I figure you always knew quite a lot about Joey's queer pals and you didn't care a bit about them until you became anxious that Joey was starting to care more for the Dago than he cared for you. You were afraid that Joey would tell the Dago kid all about the Kipinski diamond heist, which only you knew about at the time."

"Where do you get these ugly ideas?"

"They come to me."

"You've got it wrong, Harry."

"For a long time on this case I believed it was Joe the Dude and Eddie Molloy who cooked up the Kipinski caper. That fit very nicely into my notion that Joey was not capable of anything really impressive. Well, I was wrong about that. Joey had a real head on those skinny shoulders. He knew about the Forty-seventh Street Jews and their pockets full of gems, walking around, easy to take, like shooting ducks in a barrel. It was *Joey* who planned and carried out the Kipinski robbery. He did it by persuading Kipinski's partner to cooperate with him, to let Joey know when the old man would be going out with a fortune on him. The partner thought it would be a case of his claiming the insurance on two policies and then buying back the gems for resale. That was Joey's idea, too. There'd be plenty to split among his three loves, you, Vito Dacapua, and the Nazis. A grand-slam home run in the big-shot department. But, alas, big brother Wop stepped in because he didn't cotton to the idea of Joey Seldes screwing his little brother. Joey gets iced, and the stones lie uncollected where Joey'd left them."

"Why the note, Mr. Know-it-all?"

"Ah, the note. It keeps coming back to the note."

"Yes. The key *man,* and the safe combination, and—"

I cut her off with a wave of my hand. "Say that again, what you just said about the *man.*"

She looked at me as if I were crazy or suddenly gone deaf. "In the note. It began with the words, 'The key *man*—' "

"Right!" I said, slapping my forehead as if I *were* crazy. "You've just *said* it the way Joey'd *meant* it. 'The key *man.*' Not the *key* man. The *man* is the key, and all time I was figuring he was a *key*man, like a *train*man or a *door*man. I had him down as a man who handled keys. It's the man who was important in the note!"

"Well, naturally. That's obvious."

"Wrong, baby. Anyone reading that message filled with its combinations and locker number and directions on where to find the hiding place would assume, as I did, that Kenny Lambda, was a man who had a *key* to Joey's hiding place for the gems. *I* assumed wrong. You *knew* a *man* was the key to your getting the gems. You knew all about the meaning of the note, what that combination was for, who Kenny was, what you were to tell him

—up to a point—and what you were to do once Kenny retrieved Joey's goods for you from the hiding place. You knew where the diamonds were the day you came into this office and hired me to get them for you."

"That's ridiculous! If I'd known their whereabouts, I would have gone there to get them. Why should I bring you into it?"

"Because you couldn't get them. Someone had to get them for you. Kenny had to get them. Only, when you went around to see Kenny and to tell him to bring you the things from Joey's locker, you found out Kenny didn't work there anymore."

"Kenny who? Worked where? This is nonsense. If I knew where the diamonds were, I assure you I would have gotten them by myself."

"Uh, uh. They were where you couldn't get to them. They were in a locker in the basement of a private Turkish bathhouse, an exclusive and very queer club where ladies are never, ever admitted, so a man had to get them. A man had to be the key to your retrieving the gems, and Joey figured it might as well be Kenny, for whom it was natural to be going into others' lockers. Joey told Kenny that you might be coming around to pick up his belongings in the event he couldn't get them himself. When Joey was killed, you followed the instructions in Joey's half-assed attempt at cryptography and went to the Lambda Society and asked for Kenny, only to learn Kenny'd quit. At that point, you didn't know what to do. Since you couldn't get Joey's goods on your own, you decided to get some help. That's where I came in."

"I had no idea what the Lambda Society is."

"Sure you did, hon. You knew everything about your late husband's queer habits. He told you every detail. When it dawned on him that he might need you to retrieve the diamonds someday, he wrote that note for you and explained what it meant so you'd know the secret of it but no one else could without a lot of digging around."

"You are so wrong, Harry!"

"I don't think so. I had plenty of things wrong at first. I even thought you might have set Joey up for his killing. Why didn't you?"

"I'm not a killer."

"That's probably the truest thing you ever said in your whole life." I looked at her with a lot more sympathy than I would have expected of myself, seeing how she'd played me for a sucker all along. I never was a pushover for a woman's tears the way most men are and I was always able to spot when a woman was turning to tears because all else had failed, the way Gloria had attempted to use them that first day she came to see me. Then, she'd quickly recognized that tears were not my Achilles' heel and she dropped that gambit in a hurry. Now tears were in her baby-blue eyes again. "Go ahead and cry, honey," I said, reaching for my hanky. "I don't blame you. Right now, tears are about all you've got."

She grabbed my handkerchief and patted her eyes. Somehow, this time it seemed a lot more genuine. She took a breath, crumpled my hanky in her hand, and gave a quick nod of her pretty head. "All right. Yes. It was the way you just said. I did know all about what Joey had gotten himself into. I knew where the diamonds were. I was anxious that something might happen to him before he could get to them. I persuaded him to see how important it was for someone he trusted to know. I said that it ought to be me, that I was the only person he could truly trust."

"How very humble of you, doll."

"He finally realized I was right, and he explained to me about the Lambda Society and that if anything happened to him before he could get the diamonds, I should go to see Kenny, who worked there, tell him who I was, give him the combination to Joey's locker and promise him ten dollars if he'd bring me everything inside the locker."

"Ten bucks? Generous son of a bitch, your late husband."

"Then Joey was killed."

"Poor Joey."

"I waited a bit, then went to the Lambda Society and asked for Kenny. I was told he had quit his job. I was confused. I didn't know what to do."

"So you came to me."

"Not right away."

"Why not?"

"Because I never even thought about using a private detective at that point."

"When did this flash of inspiration come to you?"

She looked down at my hanky, all twisted and wrinkled from her nervous knotting and unknotting of it. Into her lap she said, "It was somebody else's idea."

"Somebody *else's?*"

Her big blues came up to me, wide, teary, terrified. "Yes."

"Whose idea?"

"Inspector Grady."

"How the hell did you get connected with him? That was dumb of you, darling."

"I had no choice, Harry."

"You had no choice?"

"He forced me to do what he said."

"Hold it, darling. You're racing too far ahead of me now. Go slow in telling me how Grady managed all this."

"He came around to my apartment and told me he knew all about Joey and the diamonds and that if I didn't do what he said to get the diamonds I would be in big trouble. Official trouble, yes. Plus the kind of trouble he said a man like him could make for me. Personal trouble. I took that as a threat on my life."

"Understandable, doll, coming from Grady."

"He said he believed I knew where Joey had hidden the diamonds and that if I didn't get them and share them with him—"

"Grady never changes his stripes, does he?" I laughed.

"I was scared, Harry. I told him everything I knew."

"So how come Grady didn't breeze in there and grab the loot?"

"He said he is under a lot of pressure, scrutiny, in the department and that it was too risky for him to try it. He said we had to get someone else to get them for us."

"Then he nominated me."

"Yes."

I laughed. "Oh, that is good! That son of a bitch. Just like him."

"You do believe me?"

"In spite of all I've learned about your respect for the truth, yes, I believe you, but only because this is so much in character for Grady that you'd have to know him to come up with a story like that. Yeah. I believe you. I can even piece together how Grady's mind was working. He knew about the diamonds because he was on the robbery investigation briefly. He was yanked for some reason. Maybe because someone in Lew Valentine's office figured Grady in proximity to that much ice would be too great a temptation. Grady hears from his mobster sources that Joey was mixed up in the caper. Then Joey is murdered downstairs. Grady is in charge of that case, which was natural. Now he wonders what's gonna happen to the stones, and that's when he comes to see you. Something like that?"

"It would seem so."

"You went along strictly because you were afraid of him?"

"Why else?" I could see she was offended by the very idea of what she thought I might have been thinking. "There was nothing between Grady and me."

"I didn't say there was, honey."

"How could you even think it?"

"Who said I was thinking there was something between Grady and you?"

"You have a cop's mind. You were thinking it."

"So you were just scared of him, not in love with him or screwing him for the fun of it. I can believe that. It's prudent to be a little scared of Grady all the time. He is a bit looney, you know, from greed. As to the chance you might blurt all this out to me, he counted on you being more afraid of him than of me, which adds up. Only now you have blurted it all out to me, baby. How come?"

"You were that close to figuring it anyway, weren't you?"

"Maybe yes, maybe no. It's flattering to me to know that you think that much of my detective work, so I'll say, Yes, I was close to it. Only now, darling, you're in the middle between the rock and the hard place. Terrified of Grady. Afraid of me because I just might have the diamonds and you have to deal with me for them. I suppose he sent you up here?"

"Yes."

"Where is he?"

"In a car downstairs."

"What's his plan?"

"If you know where the diamonds are and agree to take me to them, we go downstairs together. He'll be waiting to follow us. He'd step in when you actually picked up the stones."

"That asshole always gave himself too much credit for being an expert at tailing. He's a lousy tail. If I don't come down?"

"He assumes you're being uncooperative. He comes up."

"And you?"

"He waits until I come down before he comes up."

"Figures. No witnesses that way."

"He's a dangerous man, Harry. He seems very desperate, as if his whole world is coming apart and getting his hands on these diamonds is his last chance."

"Why was he so certain today's the day I'd have the gems?"

"He's been watching you since the day I hired you. He did it himself when his job permitted it. He had other cops tail you when he couldn't. They didn't know why they were doing it. He knows where you were last night. At that Nazi's place. He read the paper today. He connects that to the diamonds. He says you have to have them. Do you, Harry?"

"Would you answer that if you were in my shoes?"

"Harry, you have to get me out of this fix."

"I have to get *us* out of it, darling. Remember *us?*"

"You could, uh, do to him what you, uh, did to that Nazi."

I barked a laugh. "Honey, I don't just go around blasting guys."

"It would be self-defense."

"Yeah, but I don't happen to have my gun on me."

"What?"

"The cops unloaded me of my armor when they arrested me last night."

"You don't keep one here in your office?"

"I don't keep anything here that I'd miss not having around. This place is too easy to break into. It happened twice this week. I told you."

"The second time," she whispered, looking down again and twisting my hanky, "it was Grady who did it."

I had a sudden picture of Grady beating up on Sliphorn Kelly, those ham-hock fists of Grady's pummeling Slip, his fingers on Slip's throat, that grating ugly voice demanding to know where I was, where the diamonds were, and Sliphorn not knowing anything about anything except how to make pretty music out of a slide trombone.

"How do you know it was Grady?" I asked her.

"He told me. He said he'd come over here looking for you because he was sure you had the gems. He said you weren't here but some other guy was and that guy got in the way so he had to muss him up. That's when he cooked up this plan that brought me here today. You see, his men saw you the other day carrying a musical instrument case. They told Grady about it. They didn't know what to make of it. Grady added it up to the diamonds being in the case."

"Grady always was an ass."

"What do we do?"

"How afraid of him are you?"

"Petrified."

"I wish you hadn't said that. You could have said terrified or scared shitless, but not petrified. Petrified means you can't move."

"What?"

"Suppose you were to go down and tell Grady I was being uncooperative?"

"He'd come up."

"Leaving you down there alone?"

"Yes."

"So you could go into the Onyx and tell Louie you need the gun from behind the bar. I'll call down to Louie and tell him it's okay."

"Oh, Harry, I don't know if I could."

"Only way out, darling. You have to do it. Grady'll have his gun and I don't have one."

"I couldn't . . . shoot . . . him."

"No need to. Just get the drop on him while I relieve him of his gun. Easy. Ready?"

She nodded her head a couple of times, fast, like a kid about to take medicine. "I'm very frightened, Harry."

"You'll do fine, darling. You're a tough dame. You'll come through!" I showed her to the door. When she was gone, I called Ben Turner, waking him up. "Ben, get your ass and some cops up to my place as fast as you can!" I hung up before he could ask why.

I called down to the Onyx and told Louie to do what I was about to tell him without arguing. Louie knew better than to argue. Then I waited.

It wasn't long, though it seemed it, before I heard Grady's size thirteens on the stairs. A second later his belly was a shadow in the glass door. Then he was inside. "I hear you're being difficult, MacNeil," he said without preliminaries.

"You know how I am, Grady."

He closed the door and yanked out his .38. "This little showdown is overdue by a couple of years."

"Yeah, I should have shot you that day in City Hall Park."

"Stand up and move away from the desk and take off your jacket and put up your hands so's I can see your armpits."

"You know they took my gun last night."

"Guns are easy to get. You had time."

"I was sleeping all day."

"Move. Coat. Arms."

I followed his directions explicitly.

Pleased to see a holster with no gun in it, he said, "Where are the stones?"

"Not here, obviously."

"Tell me where they are."

"If I don't, you shoot me?"

"Yeah."

"That won't get you the stones."

"If I don't have the stones, I'll have the satisfaction."

"Shooting me is equal to three million in rocks?"

"Easily."

"I knew you detested me, Grady, but I'm flattered by how much."

"Where are they?"

"You wouldn't believe me if I told you."

"They were in the locker at that queer bathhouse."

"Yes, they were."

"I know you were there last night. I know you didn't have time to stash them. I know the cops didn't find them on you. So, where are they?"

"I'll never tell. Not even to Winchell."

Grady chewed his lower lip, then broke into a grin. "The runt from the *News!* Of course. He has them!"

"Ben Turner! That's a laugh."

"Get him on the phone and tell him to come over here."

"Ben sleeps days."

"It's late. He'll be at work."

"Maybe he's on assignment."

"Call him."

"By the way, where's Gloria?"

"Forget her."

"I wish you'd've told me that a couple of days ago."

"Very funny."

"Yeah, isn't it." I chuckled. Inside, I was wondering where she was. Then the phone rang. Grady jumped like a spooked horse. Then he waved the muzzle of his gun, making it plain I was to answer the phone. It was Louie with the bad news that Gloria Seldes had never come in to pick up the gun. "Thanks, Louie," I said.

"What was that?" Grady asked.

"It was Louie downstairs. He had bad news for me, good news for you."

"Call Turner," Grady said, waving the gun again.

The phone was, it seemed plain to me, my only weapon and my only chance. I flung it at Grady. It smashed him like David's rock smashed Goliath, only Goliath hadn't been holding a pistol at the time and David was not hit very painfully in the shoulder as I was by a shot that Grady got off even as he was stumbling back, the phone in his face. Luckily, I got to the gun he dropped before he did.

Like any good cop, Grady carried a second pistol, a beauty of a derringer, stuffed in his sock.

I killed him with a .38 slug through the chest before he got the derringer past his kneecap.

Ben arrived about two minutes before the cops. Usually the N.Y.P.D. would have responded a lot sooner to a call from a citizen reporting trouble, but coordination between the cops and the men from the Department of Streets was not very good on days after big snowfalls.

I'd been in a bed, bandaged and fed, with truly awful hospital food at Roosevelt for over an hour before Lew Valentine barged into my room seeking explanations.

24

Jazzin' at the Onyx

Sliphorn Kelly died the night before I was released from the hospital. Mine was only a two-day stay. I could have been out sooner, but even Lewis J. Valentine was not able to make things happen that fast, not even when I pressed upon him the urgency with which I felt I had to act in order to put my hands on the Kipinski diamonds. Gruffly, Valentine said, "The time has come for you to leave this matter to the police, Harry. We'll retrieve the diamonds. Just tell us where they are."

"I need to do it on my own, Lew."

"There's no way I can permit it, Harry," said the Police Commissioner.

"If you send cops after the diamonds, you'll never get them. I guarantee you. I have a chance at it. You give me a chance. A couple of hours. If I come up empty, I turn it all over to you."

"The Little Flower is very upset about this already."

"Assure the Mayor that everything's under control. Tell him to try a little of that patience and fortitude bullshit he's always espousing."

Valentine broke into a laugh. "You tell him. I've not the courage to."

He was about to leave when I called to him to wait. "What about Gloria? Did you find her?"

"She had one foot on the Twentieth Century Limited, but we have her. We're holding her as a material witness."

"That is tricky and dangerous material, Lew."

"I understand, Harry," he said, leaving the room so I could get dressed and get back on the damnedest case I'd ever handled.

There was one of New York City's incomparable cold, blue, clear beautiful days outside.

Ben Turner greeted me in his borrowed *News* car. "You know" —he smiled with that great smile under that Jewish nose—"my boss, Captain Patterson, may decide to send you a bill for taxi service. Where to?"

"Uptown. Harlem. Number 250 West 134th Street."

"Ooo, that is a rough neighborhood, Harry."

"These days they're all rough, my friend. Drive on."

Kendal Johnson was not at home. He had not been home for quite a while. Not since two days after he suddenly up and quit his job at a Turkish bath downtown. Kendal Johnson, said the lady who'd lived next door to him for twenty-five years, had a stroke of luck. "Yes," she said, shaking her head in amazement and envy and admiration, "Kenny, he finally hit the big one in the policy. Do you know 'bout policy? White folks have their gamblin' casinos and horse racin', we niggers have the policy. For twenty years Kenny played the policy. He had more schemes for choosin' a number! Then a time ago, day or two before he moved, he hit it big. Said he finally found the number."

"Was it by any chance 123?"

The black woman's eyes bulged wide like a bad imitation of Aunt Jemima on the pancake boxes. "That was it! How'd you know?"

"I guessed. Did he say where he was going?"

"Kenny was a believer in the ideas of Marcus Garvey."

I grinned and looked at Ben, who broke into another of those big Jewish smiles.

"I used to argue with Kenny all the time. I said it made no sense for niggers to pack up and go to Africa. What'd Garvey mean: Back to Africa? I used to say to Kenny, 'I wasn't born in Africa. I was born in South Carolina. If I go back to where I came from, I go back to Charleston.' I used to say that to Kenny. Well, Kenny believed that Marcus Garvey Back-to-Africa stuff, and that's where he went. I was down to the dock to wave him goodbye. A big ship it was. Fancy. He sure looked happy. Only I couldn't rightly be proud of Kenny on that day."

"Why not?" Ben asked.

"Oh, I was happy that he'd made it big in the policy, but Kenny was turnin' tails and runnin', and that ain't the way we niggers should be handlin' ourselves. We got problems in this country, only we should stay right here and work at fixin' things 'stead of runnin' away. Maybe it'll take more years than I got left, but I'd never go to Africa and turn my back on things the way they are here. Understand?"

"Patience and fortitude, lady," I said, as Ben and I left to head back downtown.

It turned out that Sliphorn Kelly had family in St. Louis, and it was the family which arranged Slip's funeral out by the shores of the "ole man river" that Jerome Kern and Oscar Hammerstein II romanticized in *Show Boat* back in 1927. Still, it seemed fitting that The Street give Slip a send-off. So late one night near the end of February when The Street was quieting down and the clubs were closing, the musicians gathered at the Onyx for a jam dedicated to Sliphorn Kelly. Somebody put his trombone on a red velvet cushion on the chair Slip used to sit on when he played the Onyx, and a light shone on it so the horn glinted and gleamed prettily. Then, one after another, the really fine people in jazz, male and female, black and white, put in their say. Around five in the morning, Louie came out from in back of the bar and lifted a clarinet from the pro who'd been playing it and handed it to me. "Your turn, Mick Dick."

They told me I did okay for a big shambling red-haired ex-cop who would just as soon leave the private shamus work to someone else if there came a chance to sit in on a good jam where a non-pro Irish ex-cop clarinet-playing private eye could get in a few good licks.

That was the great thing about the Onyx. It was okay for a guy like me to jam with the greatest.

A couple of days later, the D.A. held one of those hearings that prosecutors insist on. She was there, telling all, and it came out

the way I'd figured it, the way it had to have been and how she
walked out of the office and kept going, leaving me to whatever
it was that might happen between Grady and me.

After the hearing, I never saw Gloria Seldes again.

It turned out that there was no one the D.A. could indict for
anything serious. Vitelloni Dacapua had departed the country.
There was no direct evidence to show that his big brother had
engineered the rubout at the Onyx Club. There was nothing to
pin on Herschel Ziskowitz. They never found his partner. The
D.A. was convinced Joshua Sloman had been killed accidentally,
and who did it was never located. As far as anyone could find out,
Kendal Johnson had arrived in the African country of Liberia
and vanished, as anyone could who had three million in diamonds
to finance the disappearance.

On February 28, 1935, a fire broke out in a back room of the
Onyx Club and the joint burned down. I stood across The Street
watching and feeling as if I'd been kicked in the groin. It wasn't
that my office was going up in smoke. There wasn't a hell of a
lot in there to cry over. It was because the Onyx was going. I
knew Joe Helbock would open a new Onyx, but it could never
be the same, I figured.

You can't recapture a tune that's been played, I always say.

Author's Note

As far as I know, there never was a rubout at the Onyx Club.
This story is fiction set against the reality of one of the most
fabulous city blocks of all time. Most of the historical persons
who play a part in the story were patrons of the Onyx, although
they may not have been in the places and situations in which I
have placed them for the purposes of the book, which, I hope,
touches the truth of what New York and Fifty-second Street and
America and the world were like in the 1930s, when the people of
that time had only begun to lose their innocence but didn't know
it because they were having too much fun with their last swinging
fling before World War II and the nuclear age turned America
into a superpower.

A few notes on the lives and fates of the real people in the
story:

The fabulous **Art Tatum**, born in Toledo, Ohio, in 1910, became one of the truly great jazz pianists and a model for all who
followed him. He died in Los Angeles in 1956.

Jimmie Lunceford, born in 1902, was a graduate of Fisk University, receiving his musical tuition from Paul Whiteman. Beginning in 1934, Lunceford's band was famed for having the
biggest beat in the business, thanks in large measure to great
arrangers such as Sy Oliver and Ed Wilcox. The band declined
in the 1940s, when his best sidemen left him. Lunceford died
in 1947.

Paul Pops Whiteman is still controversial. Some say his symphonic approach to jazz was never jazz at all. For a time in the early years of television, Pops had a successful TV show featuring the Whiteman orchestra. He died in Doylestown, Pennsylvania, in 1967.

George Gershwin died in Beverly Hills, California, July 11, 1937, less than two years after the triumphal premier of *Porgy and Bess*.

Walter Winchell, to whom every gossip columnist owes a debt for style and vocabulary, remained a force in New York newspapers into the 1960s. He died on February 20, 1972.

Police Commissioner **Lewis J. Valentine,** who had started as a foot patrolman with the N.Y.P.D. in 1903, retired in 1945, then served as an adviser to General Douglas MacArthur in setting up police forces in postwar Japan and Korea. He authored a book, *Night Stick,* and, beginning in 1945, hosted radio's *Gangbusters* program. Valentine died on December 16, 1947.

James John Walker, the 100th Mayor of New York, was born in New York in 1881. Dabbling in songwriting and politics, he launched his political career in 1908 as a member of the state assembly. A protégé of Alfred E. Smith, Walker was elected to the state senate. Tammany Hall backing put him in City Hall in 1925. His enormous popularity got him re-elected in 1927 with a victory over Fiorello La Guardia. "This man of rainbow charm appeared forever young in a city three hundred years old," wrote biographer Gene Fowler in *Beau James.* "One might easily discern his shortcomings, his thirst for flattery, his random bestowals of friendship and affection, but find in him no intolerance of any kind, no malice, no hypocrisy, no selfishness."

During his second administration, the Seabury Investigation uncovered widespread fraud, and fifteen charges were lodged against Walker, including income tax violations. After he resigned, Walker lived for a time in Europe—his enemies said he ran away—but returned to discover he was as beloved as ever by his city. The charges against him were later dropped. Although married and a Roman Catholic, Walker carried on a long and rather public affair with actress Betty Compton, whom he married after his wife divorced him.

Once, at the depths of the scandal swirling around him, a friend sought to console him by saying, "Everyone is for you, Jim. All the world loves a lover." Walker replied, "You are mistaken. What the world loves is a winner." He died in 1946. His epitaph was spoken by restaurateur Toots Shor. Peering at Walker in his coffin, Toots cried out, "Jimmy! Jimmy! When you walked into the room you brightened up the joint!"

Fiorello H. La Guardia served as Mayor until 1945. He was one of the chief backers of a new charter for the city. During the war he became director of the U.S. Office of Civil Defense and co-ordinator of the U.S.-Canadian Joint Defense Committee. In 1946 he was named special ambassador to Brazil and was later appointed director general of the U.N. Relief and Rehabilitation Agency. His autobiography was published posthumously. La Guardia was famous for his Sunday evening radio broadcasts over the city's station. During a 1945 newspaper strike he made it a policy to read the funny papers to the children who tuned in. Chiding Commissioner Valentine during one of his broadcasts, La Guardia noted that Dick Tracy was a very svelte detective. "Lew Valentine," he asked, "why do our detectives get fat, I wonder?" La Guardia died in his beloved New York City on September 20, 1947. It's said that the silence was so complete on the day of his funeral that when the hearse rode through the streets you could hear the click of the traffic lights as they changed.

Owen Madden was born in Liverpool, England, in 1892 and was brought to the United States in 1903. As a member of the notorious Gopher Gang he ran up forty-four arrests by age twenty-one. He was to be a survivor in the shark-infested waters of New York gangdom. He was convicted of murder in 1914. Paroled, he emerged from Sing Sing to become one of New York's top gangsters through Prohibition and the early 1930s. Owen—Owney the Killer—Madden died of natural causes in 1964 in Hot Springs, Arkansas.

The Onyx was rebuilt, opening its doors on July 23, 1935, at 62 West Fifty-second. It was relocated in later years at 57 West

Fifty-second. I should note that I borrowed the atmosphere and four of the real events of the Onyx for the purposes of this story: the night Utah put Repeal over; the historic jam session that Harry MacNeil sat in on; the "big instruments" wager; and the scene reported to be the impetus behind the writing of the hit song "The Music Goes Round and Round" by Mike Riley and Ed Farley.

As for The Street of Jazz, it is no more. Only "21" remains, and it is not a bastion of jazz. It is one of the most fashionable restaurants in New York. And expensive. The Street is beginning to be memorialized in a small way by the placing of plaques in the sidewalk on the north side near Sixth Avenue to commemorate some of the great names who jammed in that fabulous block in its heyday.

I am greatly indebted to the scholarship of others in my work on the historical aspects of The Street, especially a superb "oral history" by Arnold Shaw, *The Street That Never Slept*, Coward, McCann & Geohegan, Inc., New York, 1971; and to the great newspapers and columnists of the era, including Winchell, Bob Considine, Danton Walker, Earl Wilson, Louis Sobol, and Robert Sylvester, author of *No Cover Charge* and *Notes of a Guilty Bystander*.

Finally, if there is any authenticity in the mood of what I've written about a period that was at its peak at about the time I was born, it can be attributed in large part to the 1930s jazz records I put on my stereo when approaching the task of writing.

Probably, if I had kept the stereo off and the records on the shelf, I would have written the book a lot quicker! Many days were filled with much music and no writing, I confess.

About the Author

H. Paul Jeffers was only a few months old when the events in *Rubout at the Onyx* took place, and the fabulous Street of Jazz was only a memory when he made his home in New York City and began writing books and working in television and radio, including stints in the news departments of ABC, NBC, and CBS, where he works at present in a building across the street from the spot where the Onyx flourished in the 1930s and '40s. His books include, *The Adventure of the Stalwart Companions*, a Sherlock Holmes thriller set in New York City in 1880; *Wanted by the FBI; See Parris and Die; Sex in the Executive Suite;* and several young-adult histories and biographical sketches from American history. He also has been a teacher of journalism in several colleges and universities, a Fulbright lecturer in Thailand, a record producer, and a playwright.